Murder At The Pickwick Hotel

MISS MARKHAM MYSTERY SERIES
BOOK EIGHT

JULIET E. SIDONIE

Murder At The Pickwick Hotel

MISS MARKHAM MYSTERY SERIES
BOOK EIGHT

Image printed with permission by the Kansas City Public Library Missouri Valley Special Collections

JULIET E. SIDONIE

Murder at the Pickwick Hotel - A Miss Markham Mystery

Library of Congress Control Number: ___Applied________________________

ISBN (hardcover): 979-8-9941127-6-2

ISBN (paperback): 979-8-9941127-7-9

Kansas City Shuffle Book Reviews:

"In the "Murder at the Pickwick Hotel" the author, Juliet Sidonie, takes Deloris on an Adventure to prove that a suicide is in fact a murder. It's captivating to visualize Deloris and her friends as they visit different areas and homes in 1936 Kansas City. Her bravery and curiosity help the reader to follow along during each step of her journey."

— **Stella All**

"Murder at the Pickwick Hotel" is a well-crafted mystery that combines plot twists and rich character development. It's a must-read for fans of the genre and anyone who enjoys unraveling complex mysteries within a vividly drawn historical context. Like on all of this author's series, she includes added information in the front and back of her books that make her stories that much more interesting."

— **Rosie Russell of "Books by Rose**

"Miss Markham finds herself on one of her most personal who-done-it mysteries yet! 'in more ways than one' When a close friend from back home is found dead in his hotel room ruled a suicide, she must find all the clues and facts he left behind to prove it wasn't suicide but cold-blooded murder!"

— **Racheal Shatswell**

Acknowledgements

We would like to thank our families for their support, suggestions and help. Thanks especially go to our beta readers: Elden Dilks, Kristie Zorn, Joyce Henkins, Gail Metcalf Schartel, Racheal Shatswell, Judy Pelletier, Rosie Russell, Stella All, Lesley Couch, and Jo Ann Day for their feedback, suggestions, and especially for catching errors.

Thank you to Sara McClure for copy editing, Carolyn Day for the book cover and formatting of the book.

Finally, thank you to the Kansas City Public Library, Missouri Valley Special Collections, for permission to use the postcard image of the Pickwick Hotel on our book cover.

This book is dedicated to Doris Markham, our inspiration and role model, and loosely based upon the book Miss Kansas City Kitty Doris Markham's Story.

Table of Contents

Preface
The Pickwick Hotel

TThe Pickwick Plaza included an eleven-story, 500-room Pickwick Hotel, a seven-story Pickwick Office Building, a large public parking garage, and the Pickwick-Greyhound Union Bus Terminal. They all opened August 1, 1930 with an all-day celebration hosted by the Pickwick-Greyhound Bus Company. One newspaper article said the Pickwick had 300 rooms, another said there were 400 rooms and two at its opening said there were 500 rooms. Not confusing at all. I'm going with 500 rooms, because that was reported at its opening by two newspapers.

On the same day, KMBC radio opened its new offices on the eleventh floor of the Pickwick Hotel. At the time, the Pickwick Plaza's opening made it the largest mixed complex west of the Mississippi and, as reported in the Kansas City Journal Post, the world's largest bus terminal. The hotel's proximity to downtown government buildings, the bus terminal and business offices made it easy for travelers to conduct business in one location. (A composite of articles taken from the Kansas City Journal-Post, Kansas City, Missouri—Thursday, July 31, 1930, Pages 3 and 27)

The Kansas City Public Library, Missouri Valley Special Collections, has this blurb about it.

> *A news story of March 9, 1923, announced that negotiations in progress for some weeks resulted this p.m. in an agreement of the terms of a $2,950,000 bond issue to finance the immediate erection of the*

interurban station and a 10-story office building at the northeast corner of 10th and McGee. The project occupied the entire block from 9th to 10th on McGee. C.C. Peters was president of the Interurban Central Station Company. (He was also secretary of the Emery-Bird-Thayer department store.) It was the largest project in Downtown Kansas City at the time, and when completed was considered the largest bus terminal in the nation. Five million dollars was spent to build the facility, which included a 300-room hotel, lunchroom and dining room. There was a ballroom seating 600 for meals, which catered to conventions and meetings. Dedication of the facility was celebrated by a huge crowd on the evening of Aug. 1, 1930. Charles F. Wren, president of the Pickwick Greyhound Lines, made the presentation speech and the city's acceptance was given by Councilman Ruby D. Garrett. A bottle of ginger ale was cracked over the front bumper of the first bus to leave the station by the queen of the day, six-year-old Betty Blanche Benningfield, 7205 Madison. By 1950, three major bus lines operated from the terminal: the Southwestern Greyhound Lines, Overland Greyhound Lines of Omaha, and the Crown Coach Lines of Joplin, Mo. Eight other lines also used the depot. Later [in 1950] the dining room in French decor was [remodeled] and opened. The hotel closed in October 1968. Today Sam's Pickwick Garage occupies the old bus station. The old Pickwick Hotel, as pictured, has become the Royal Towers Apartments with cafeteria service for residents and the public in the former Pickwick Hotel dining room. Kansas City Times, June 20, 1980.

To my knowledge, no murder took place at the Pickwick Hotel. There were several suicides, including one where the deceased registered at the Pickwick Hotel as David Kerns on February 13, 1936. I hope his family will forgive me for taking liberties with his name.

The Ship

The Ship, originally located at 411 East 10th Street in Kansas City, opened Friday, September 6, 1935, and closed on November 25, 1995. It gave its patrons the feeling of being on board an actual ship and offered chicken and steak dinners. It also had a cocktail lounge. Several of the fixtures from the original Ship are used in the new location at 1221 Union Avenue, Kansas City, MO 64101, that opened in 2004.

An article in the Kansas City Journal-Post on Saturday, September 7, 1935, on page 7 under the headline "Night Club Notes" described The Ship this way:

> *"Cabareters who keep up with the latest developments are talking about the unique new downtown spot, The Ship. It offers no entertainment and no music, but one may cruise there in a real nautical atmosphere. At no slight expense, the place has been rigged by Mark Creehan, the skipper, to give the illusion of being on shipboard. It does it perfectly, even to the seascapes flashing past the portholes and the sound effects of splashing waves. The food and beverages are strictly of 'captain's table' quality."*

This book, Murder at the Pickwick Hotel, was originally to be our first book in the series, but we decided to start in 1931 with Murder Among Friends and build back stories for the characters.

List of Characters

ANNIE BAILEY– Deloris's best friend. She has a quiet demeanor and is often wrangled into escapades with Deloris that she normally wouldn't get involved in. She is a reporter with the Kansas City Post newspaper. Annie is pretty with a cute round face and a few freckles sprinkled across her nose. Her electric blue eyes complement her inquiring mind and contrast perfectly with her curly strawberry-blonde hair.

AUSTIN MARTIN– Deloris's childhood friend who is a detective with the Kansas City Police Department. He is six feet tall with an athletic build, wavy blonde hair and sapphire-blue eyes.

BLANCHE KERNS– David Kerns's mother. Mrs. Kerns is a widow with a certain air of authority and superiority. She has angered her share of people through the years with her temperamental attitude that makes her difficult to get along with people other than a few of her social group of friends.

ESTHER HERNANDEZ– Mrs. Kerns's maid who works hard with minimal compensation. Esther is short and a little round. Her hair is salt and pepper, and her brown eyes show a sadness of love lost.

JOSE GOMEZ– Esther's brother as well as Blanche's gardener, landscaper, and chauffeur. Jose is about five feet six inches tall with dark brown eyes, a mustache, and almost totally gray hair.

CECILIA GLOVER– Thelma's newest boarder. Cecilia is a tall woman with a very thin build, curly brown hair and brown eyes to match. She had just moved to the Kansas City area from Casper, Wyoming, when she took a job as a seamstress at the Donnelly Garment Company. She took the room that had formerly belonged to Edith Wellington. Edith moved out when she married Big Jim Anderson.

CLARENCE MARKHAM– Deloris's second oldest brother, who stayed on the farm to help her parents run the farm. He is about five feet ten inches tall, with brown hair and blue-green eyes.

DR. DAVID KERNS– The victim. David is six feet two inches tall, with kind blue eyes that stood out from behind his spectacles. He kept his brown hair cut short. Dr. Kerns is in a medical practice with Dr. Jeremiah Browne but just received an offer to collaborate with a famous researcher, Dr. Myron S. Cramer, in another state.

DELORIS (DEDE) MARKHAM– Amateur sleuth. Deloris is five feet two inches with violet-blue eyes and a petite figure. She was little but mighty. By day, she works at the Kansas City Police Department switchboard; by night, she works as a server at one of the local supper clubs.

DR. DONALD JOHNSON– Fired from his job working on the lucrative James & James research project with Dr. Cramer and blamed David Kerns for replacing him.

DOROTHY BRAXTON– Bank teller at the Jameson Farmers' Bank in Jameson, Missouri. She was Dorothy Smith and recently married.

ELDEN DOUGLAS–Chief of the Kansas City Police Department. Chief Douglas is a 60-year-old man of average height, with a slow but methodical walk. His almost bald head has the typical semi-circular patch of gray hair, and his deep blue eyes can measure up a speaker in a matter of minutes with a piercing stare. Chief Douglas has seen the best and worst of humanity in his forty years on the force; that shows in every wrinkle on his face and slightly stooped posture.

EVELYN "EVIE" DAVIS–Evie lives next door to Thelma with her parents and younger sister, Nora. Twenty-year-old Evie is very cute with her deep dimples and long brown hair. She is a fashionista with an extensive wardrobe of clothes for every occasion. She takes classes at the Edna Marie Dunn Fashion Design School.

GEORGE PACKARZ– A bellhop at the Pickwick Hotel and one of Deloris's boyfriends. George is about five feet nine inches with dark brown hair, blue eyes, and a dimple in his chin.

GRACE "GRACIE" BURNETT– Lives at Thelma's and takes classes at Kansas City University. She works at the Kansas City Police Department switchboard on weekends. She is a cool, calm and collected young woman who knows exactly what she wis going to do with her life. She has goals and she works hard to meet each of them. She has shoulder length blonde hair that she curls with a curling iron to fit around her hats. Her emerald green eyes sparkle with light, joy, and optimism.

JAMES "BIG JIM" ANDERSON– A detective at the Kansas City Police Department. Big Jim is over six feet tall, with brown hair and green eyes. He is a former Marine who has mastered the art of the intimidating stare. Austin is his partner. He recently married Edith Wellington, now Mrs. Anderson, a chemistry teacher at Kansas City University.

DR. JEREMIAH BROWNE– Dr. David Kerns's business partner. Dr. Browne fancies himself a Casanova. He is known to be tactless with his patients, except the pretty ones. Dr. Browne's wife, Alice, recently committed suicide, as did her father, Dr. Joseph Walters.

JOEY CRABTREE – A young, green-behind-the-ears police officer who works with Austin Martin and Big Jim Anderson. Joey is about five feet eight inches tall with brown hair, blue-green eyes and brown hair.

LENORA "NORA" DAVIS– Lives next door to Thelma with her parents, Ben and Charlotte Davis, and older sister, Evie. Nora is a beautiful girl with medium length blondish-brown hair that she wears in a tight bun. She has gray eyes and dimples like her sister. She walks with the grace of a ballerina. She is finishing her senior year in high school and takes ballet lessons at the Ruth Shafton Studio of Dance. In the fall, she will transition to the Conservatory of Music's professional ballet program.

LEOTA JONES– Another boarder at Thelma's boarding house. Leota is about five feet two with a medium build. She wears her short, straight, mousy brown hair in a 1920s pixie style, making her look like a flower from an old bouquet. She works as a maid at the President Hotel and babysits Thelma's daughters. She has a cat that has recently turned very mean. Deloris is also allergic to the cat and tries to steer clear of it when she is home.

LES WELLS– One of Deloris's boyfriends from Independence. He works at Polly's Pop and was recently promoted to manager of the line. Les is about six feet tall with an athletic build. He has blondish-brown hair and blue eyes.

LUCILLE "LUCY" MCCOY– David Kerns's ex-girlfriend who is now dating Bob Scott. Lucy never really got over David Kerns and is still in love with him. She is a love-starved woman who could be swayed with a few kind words. Lucy has a secret past that no one knows about.

DR. MYRON S. CRAMER– A famous researcher with the James & James Research Institute. He is looking for researchers to help him investigate the effects of Blue Mass on patients.

PRISCILLA HEARST– Neighbor across the street from David Kerns's house.

REBECCA BRADFORD– A sketch artist at the Kansas City Police Department who also teaches at the Kansas City Art Institute. Rebecca is about five feet seven inches tall with long brown hair and green eyes.

ROBERT "BOB" SCOTT– Former sergeant in the U.S. Army who now works at a local steel mill and is dating Lucy McCoy. He can get volatile if someone messes with his girl.

ROY MARKHAM– Deloris's oldest brother, who is good friends with Dr. David Kerns. Roy is about five feet eleven inches tall with a slender build, blue eyes, and an almost totally bald head. He is a recent widower. His wife, Bert, died a few days after childbirth the year before. The babies were twin boys, one stillborn and the other one dying a day later.

THELMA WEBB– Deloris's divorced sister, who has two children and rents rooms to single females. Thelma is four feet eleven inches in height and a little round. She has freckles and short red hair. Thelma works at the local egg factory through the week and is a cook at a cafe on weekends. Deloris lives with her, as do Anne Bailey, Gracie Burnett, Cecilia Glover, and Leota Jones. People make a mistake, because of her quiet nature, that she is a pushover, but when you mess with her family—watch out.

Prologue: Valentine's Day, 1936

Was it suicide? Or was it murder? If it was murder, who did it? Those are the questions Deloris wanted answered. Deloris considered herself a pretty good detective with a knack for cutting through misdirection and seeing the truth with a type of intuition for solving crimes. She is a brunette with violet eyes, a knockout figure and good-looking gams. She is short and feisty, with a love of puzzles, excitement, and has an inquisitive mind.

Today, Friday, February 14, 1936, should have been a day filled with love and romance, but someone decided to turn it into a day of grief and pain.

Deloris worked part-time mornings at the Kansas City Police Department switchboard at a job Austin Martin — a good friend of hers from her hometown and a police detective ---helped her get.

On Friday morning, she took a call at the switchboard that a man was found dead at the Pickwick Hotel, 9th and McGee. The voice on the other end reported, "The man is not breathing and does not need medical attention. Call the coroner."

"May I have your name, please?" Deloris asked.

With authority, the voice answered, "My name is Detective Elbert Floyd, and it looks like he offed himself with poison."

"Will you be there when the police arrive to answer questions?"

"Look, sweetheart, as I said before, my name is DETECTIVE Elbert Floyd, and I work here at the hotel as a detective, so I know the routine. I'll be here." His voice dripped with mockery and amusement.

"Yes, sir," Deloris replied and quickly rang down to the front desk of the police department, to relay the information.

Since the Pickwick Hotel opened in 1930, there had already been several suicides: people jumping from one of the top-floor balconies or shooting themselves, but there hadn't been a death by poisoning. Three suicides had happened within a 48-hour period. Was the Pickwick cursed, or was it just bad luck that people stayed in its luxurious atmosphere for one last hurrah before taking their lives? It was a naive assumption that this death was from suicide and was being treated as such.

Later that day, after work, when Deloris was in her bedroom, she heard the phone ring downstairs. Since she was the only person home at that moment, she ran to answer it. Gingerly picking up the receiver, she was careful not to nick her newly polished nails.

"Hello."

Austin was at the other end of the line. He told her the victim had been identified as Dr. David Kerns, their mutual friend. David was from Jameson, the same small town as Deloris and Austin. Deloris couldn't believe her ears; she was in shock.

Annie Bailey, who also rented a room from Deloris's sister, Thelma Webb, came home excited for her Valentine date, but seeing Deloris on the phone, she slipped up to her room to get ready. Annie stopped halfway up the stairs and turned to mouth, "Are you okay?"

Deloris nodded with tears in her eyes and waved her on.

"I'm sorry, Deloris," Austin consoled her over the phone.

"It looks like suicide; David left a note."

"That can't be," she protested, shaking her head. "I just talked with David yesterday."

"How did he seem mentally to you?" Austin asked.

"He had plans to take a job in New York City and was excited at the opportunity to work with this doctor at James and James."

Austin sighed. "Yes, I find it hard to believe he committed suicide. Look, I'm going to look into it as if it is a murder, unless I find overwhelming evidence it was a suicide, but don't tell anyone. Okay?"

"Okay. You should know that he was complaining of numbness in his left hand and was feeling a little nauseated, but was going home to take some Pepto-Bismol before continuing with his plans for the evening. He almost forgot our lunch date, but I figured it was because he was preoccupied with the new job and busy winding down his practice," Deloris related.

"Really?" Austin sounded thoughtful. "When did you say the two of you talked?"

"Yesterday at noon at the Woolworth's lunch counter," Deloris replied with a catch in her throat. "He was going to the university library to collect some research that afternoon, and then meet that evening with a famous medical researcher from New York."

Tears flowed, and Deloris shook her head. It made little sense. Just yesterday, David was so excited about his future. A man contemplating suicide doesn't talk about the future and his dreams for changing the world. "Austin, how can anyone believe David killed himself?"

There was silence on the line for a second, and then Austin

sighed again. "Besides the note, one guest on the same floor reported walking past David's door and seeing a woman there arguing with him. It sounded like a lover's spat, they said."

"That must have been Lucy McCoy, but he broke up with her months ago. Anyway, who talks about their future and then commits suicide? I..." Deloris started.

Austin cut her off. "Jim and I will look into it. David was my pal, too. Remember?" He paused. "There's something else, Deloris. He left two letters. One addressed to his mother and one to you."

"To me?" Deloris gasped, dumbfounded.

"Look, can you come in this afternoon? You can read the letter and tell us everything David wrote."

Deloris agreed and said goodbye, but when she prepared to hang up, she found the fingernail polish had dried with her hair caught in it, leaving her trapped with the earpiece up to her ear. She was stuck and had to yell for help. Annie came running downstairs to see what she was shouting about. There was Deloris sitting at the telephone table with her hand holding the phone earpiece up to her ear.

"I need your help! I'm stuck," Deloris pleaded. "My fingernail polish dried with my hair in it."

Annie started laughing and ran to get some scissors to help cut her out of her dilemma. When she returned and saw the tears in Deloris's eyes and her distraught face, she asked, "What's wrong, DeDe? Why are you crying?"

Deloris told her about the phone call and David's death. Annie listened with deep concern. "Oh, my gosh! He's my doctor!"

"Mine too," Deloris cried. She eyed Annie as she approached with the scissors, cautiously adding, "Please try not to cut any more than absolutely necessary."

"I won't."

When Annie finished, Deloris stood up and thanked her. Then she ran upstairs on wobbly legs and just barely made it to the bathroom, where she washed her face, but the tears wouldn't stop. She returned to her bedroom and collapsed on her bed, where she allowed herself to let loose with sobs and tears.

Annie knocked softly on the door and stepped inside. "I'm really sorry, Deloris. I know you were close to Dr. Kerns. Are you going to be okay?" she asked.

"I don't know. I just need to be alone right now," Deloris replied without lifting her face from the pillow.

"Okay, but if you need me for anything, anything at all, just let me know."

"You go on and enjoy your date. I have to work tonight anyway," Deloris said through sniffles.

Annie nodded and closed the door quietly behind her. Deloris alone in her room, she grieved the tremendous loss, replaying memories of David in her head. Thirty-year-old Dr. David Kerns was tall and slender with dark brown hair and blue eyes. His soft-spoken, kind demeanor and listening skills made him popular with his patients and everyone who met him. Everyone but one person, apparently.

Chapter One

Dr. David Kerns

Dr. David Kerns was a source of pride for his mother and the entire town of Jameson, even though they no longer lived there. He and his mother, Mrs. Blanche Kerns, had moved to Kansas City in the early 1920s, where he received his undergraduate degree and stayed on to attend medical school in General Hospital's program. He and his mother remained in Kansas City when he started his medical practice, although he bought a house and moved out of his mother's a year later.

After moving to Kansas City, Blanche Kerns never looked back at her previous life in rural Missouri. She entered the Kansas City social scene with brute force, insisting she always got her way, and made her share of enemies. No one's opinion mattered but hers. Blanche's enemies increased almost daily. So, it was no wonder her son moved out and distanced himself.

After graduating from Jameson High School in 1931, Deloris settled in Kansas City, Missouri, too. Before she moved, her big brother, Roy Markham, a close friend and classmate of David's, sent him a letter asking him to look after his little sister in the big city. David agreed to be her acting big brother with Austin, who had been asked by her other brother, Clarence, to look after her. Deloris had so many big brothers that it was hard for her to get away with anything, but she still kept Austin on his toes. Austin was a crackerjack detective and had solved many cases, but he would often get annoyed with Deloris for horning in on his territory. Just once, he would like to see if he could solve a crime without her help. But since she was so good, he had often elicited her help.

When Deloris got to the city, she looked David up and called him to plan a meeting. David hardly knew Deloris in school because he was so much older, but she remembered him. To him, she was still a little girl who was always trying to follow him and her big brother around. Now she was all grown up, and he saw her as a young woman ready to take on the world, but still needing protection from it.

David Kerns was homefolk, a friend in a city full of strangers, scammers and scoundrels, and a good listener, too. Deloris and David soon developed a comfortable rapport, like a brother and sister. They became good friends and often made plans to have lunch on Thursdays after she got off work at the switchboard. Sometimes, Austin joined them.

Deloris didn't remember that David had gorgeous eyes that stood out from behind his spectacles; they were the bluest eyes she had ever seen. Once upon a time, every girl in school had a crush on him, as did Thelma, even though she was a few years younger and he hardly noticed her either. David was the captain of the high school basketball team and president of his class. His mother tried to discourage him from getting attached to any girl because she believed he was destined for greatness. She was in control of his life and didn't want anyone or anything to get in her way. David was her ticket to fortune, happiness, and high society.

Luckily, David inherited his father's demeanor rather than his mother's, and he saw himself as a protector of the unprotected. He aspired to make the world a better place and to save his patients, especially the pregnant ones, from dying.

David and his slightly older business partner, Dr. Jeremiah Browne, were in practice together at Browne, Kerns and

Associates. Lucky for David, when he was looking for a place to start his medical practice, Dr. Browne had an opening when his former partner, Dr. Joseph Walters III, suddenly committed suicide. His suicide, much like David's, surprised everyone and upset Thelma tremendously.

If Dr. Walters had not died, David would not have otherwise been able to start his practice. Dr. Walters was also Dr. Browne's father-in-law and was popular with his patients. David inherited all of Dr. Walters' patients and added several more.

Deloris had an epiphany. "Wait a minute," she said to herself, sitting straight up in bed. "That's right, Dr. Walters committed suicide, too. Didn't David mention that his wife, Alice, had also committed suicide? Coincidence? I think not," Deloris said aloud to no one. Like the Pickwick, those were a few too many suicides.

Deloris's thoughts returned to David again. She always looked forward to their Thursday lunches because she felt she could tell him anything, whether it was about her frustrations with her bosses or boyfriends or whatever. David Kerns was a good listener in a true big brother sort of way. Deloris was a good listener, too, and people enjoyed sharing their stories with her as well. She and David had a comfortable rapport, but their relationship was not romantic. They often swapped stories like two schoolchildren. David told her about his former girlfriend, Lucy, cheating on him with one of his patients, Bob Scott, which was why he broke off their relationship.

Deloris and David occasionally went to dinner when David wasn't dating anyone and he just wanted to go out, or when he had a medical conference event in the evening that required him to have a date. Twice on these evenings, David spotted Lucy and Bob when he was with Deloris, but was able to avoid meeting them. One time, he and Deloris were exiting the Italian Gardens as Lucy and Bob Scott were entering Johnnie Walker's bar down the street on the opposite side. He pointed them out to her as he guided Deloris in the opposite direction to avoid an altercation in the street with Lucy or Bob. He said breaking it off with Lucy was the smartest thing he ever did, but if she saw him, she would make a big scene or start flirting with him. It made him uncomfortable and he was sure it was to make Bob jealous. He was certain she would make it uncomfortable for Deloris, too.

David also shared with Deloris his frustrations about his mother dominating his life. He was also concerned about her health. He noticed she had become very forgetful and was sick more often than usual, and she wouldn't listen to his advice on taking care of herself. He also told Deloris of his frustrations with his patients—that is, what he could tell her without breaching doctor-patient confidentiality — he never used their names. Then there was his business partner, Dr. Jeremiah Browne, who he believed seemed anxious, as if there was something going on.

David often traveled to medical conferences all over the world, and he always had the most interesting stories to share when he returned. One day Deloris wanted to travel like David.

Deloris went through her memories to recall more details when she and David met for lunch that past Thursday. He had told her he was going to collaborate with the famous researcher Dr. Myron S. Cramer to investigate the hazards of medicines in pregnant women, including pilula hydrargyri or Blue Mass, a common prescription for many ailments such as constipation, melancholy, and morning sickness. Blue Mass and its mercury compound were suspected of causing people to scratch until their skin was raw and to move around with halting movements—like they were being chased by a bee. He mentioned other symptoms, but those were the ones Deloris remembered because she thought it was so strange, yet somehow familiar.

"Could people be misdiagnosed with St. Vitus' Dance when it was really mercury poisoning?" she had asked. "My parents told me I was diagnosed with St. Vitus' Dance when I was six."

"No," he said. "St. Vitus' Dance results from a streptococcus infection, not mercury poisoning."

"Well, I was just wondering if it was possible," she said, feeling a little deflated and embarrassed by her ignorance.

He smiled and consoled her before stating, "Even President Lincoln claimed the mercury caused him to act crazy, so he stopped taking it before he ran for president."

David told her that her sister-in-law, Bert, however, may have died from an overdose of Blue Mass. He felt he owed it to Roy, Deloris's older brother, to learn more about its hazards. He was a scientist as much as he was a doctor, and while research wouldn't bring Bert back, it might save another woman's life.

Deloris reached out to touch David's hand. "I'm sure Bert would be honored to know that you were researching Blue Mass because of her." That's when she noticed his hand shaking uncontrollably, and it concerned her, but she said nothing.

David explained that Dr. Cramer chose him to join his team because of an article he wrote in a respected medical journal regarding his observations about pregnant women and miscarriages and the maternal mortality rate. He cited several specific instances that he recorded from the hospital archives, and noted his personal experience with it dating back to Deloris's sister-in-law. Bert's death was when he first realized the potential dangers of Blue Mass, David continued, telling her that Dr. Myron Cramer was intrigued by his research. He had been impressed with David's credentials and the careful notes he took on each case, and said David's practical experience was much-needed on his research team.

Deloris remembered the palpable excitement in David's voice as he told her about the research. She could still see his eyes light up as he talked. His words came at a fast pace as he told her about his expected future and plans to move to New York, and asked Deloris if she would check in on his mother and his house from time to time. He also said he had plans to meet Dr. Cramer at the Pickwick Hotel that evening to discuss their research. They had a lot to go over, so he would also get a room there so they could resume their talks early the next morning over breakfast.

He then told Deloris that Dr. Browne would cover both of their patients while he worked for the next three years on the project in New York. Seeing the concerned look on Deloris's face, he added that they also had plans to bring in a new resident doctor to help with the load. Deloris was happy for David, but she didn't like the idea of him being so far away or going to Dr. Browne for her medical needs.

"Hopefully the new doctor will be better," she told him, and that was the last thing she said to dear David before he left to look something up at the library.

Deloris didn't like Dr. Browne, because when she turned twenty-one three years ago in 1933, she wanted to get an evening job serving alcohol. She heard she could make more money doing that, but she needed to get her server's permit first, which required a complete checkup. She could have asked David, but just couldn't bring herself to have David give her an examination and see her naked, so she made the appointment with Dr. Browne. He only half listened to her when she told him it was just to get a server's permit and nothing was really wrong with her. He insisted on a complete examination, anyway. After the examination, she vowed never to go to him again. He made her feel uncomfortable, as if he was enjoying it more than he should. She went home and took a long bath to wash away the experience. From that point on, Deloris always avoided Dr. Browne and went to David even if it was for something minor. Thankfully, she had nothing seriously wrong health-wise requiring a complete examination. If that happened, she would just go to another doctor across town.

Chapter Two

Boardinghouse Discussions

Deloris thought about how David Kerns's death would affect everyone in the boardinghouse. Several of the boarders, including Thelma herself, went to Browne, Kerns and Associates, having been a patient of Dr. Walters for years. He even delivered both of Thelma's babies. Dr. Walters was a good doctor, and Thelma often lamented losing him as her doctor after his death two years before. She told Deloris that she didn't like Dr. Browne or his bedside manner, but she still went to him instead of Dr. Kerns since David was still the boy, she had a crush on in high school and who hung out with their older brother Roy. She couldn't think about David seeing her naked, plus she didn't want to hurt Dr. Browne's feelings since all of Dr. Walters' other patients went to Dr. Kerns and not him. She wasn't the only one who didn't like Dr. Browne.

Deloris remembered a conversation not too long ago at Thelma's dinner table about the different doctors and how everyone there all went to the Brown, Kerns and Associates office. Someone mentioned that they were going to see Dr. Kerns the next day. Then Leota Jones, another of Thelma's boarders, spoke up and said that she was going to see him the next day, too. Thelma said it reminded her that she needed to make an appointment with Dr. Browne soon. Leota responded that she had been a patient of Dr. Browne's, but when Dr. Kerns started, she gladly switched to him. "He is so handsome, and he listens to me. He really listens."

"He does listen and is so patient," Annie agreed. "I saw him talking to an elderly lady in the waiting room who obviously had dementia. She was becoming agitated because she couldn't remember what she wanted to tell him. He calmed her down with his soothing voice."

Gracie Burnett, another boarder who worked at the KCPD switchboard with Deloris, chimed in, "Dr. Browne never listens to me or my health concerns. He is always in a hurry to get to the next patient, and he also makes me feel uncomfortable. But with Dr. Kerns, I feel calm and relaxed. He takes his time to find out what is wrong."

"That is so true," everyone at the table agreed.

"I'm going to see Dr. Kerns about my consumption," Leota said.

Leota Jones was generally quiet and shy, seldom talking to anyone except her cat. Deloris assumed she found it hard to express herself, but this night she was actually engaging in the conversation. At Thelma's, her quiet reserve was a welcome relief from the chaotic house with five boarders and Thelma's two daughters, ages nine and ten, who would run around chasing each other, arguing over one toy or another. Babysitting the girls was one of Leota's household tasks to reduce the cost of renting her room. She often took them to the park to play. Besides babysitting, she also worked as a maid at the President Hotel. When David came to the house for dinner, to stop by and say hello, or to pick Deloris up for one of their outings, Deloris could tell that Leota had a crush on him, too. Occasionally, when David Kerns came to dinner at Thelma's house, Leota would ask him a barrage of medical questions. He politely answered each one before finally saying that she should come by his office the next day and he'd write her a prescription. Deloris was fairly certain that Dr. Kerns often gave her placebos to placate her fears.

“Are you sure you have consumption, Leota?” Deloris asked with a knowing smile. Leota tended to mention an illness she had read about in the paper or had heard someone else becoming sick from, then it would become her symptoms and illness.

“Well, I’ve got something,” she said defiantly. “I need to go see Dr. Kerns,” she repeated emphatically, shoving her chair back and storming off to her room.

Cecilia Glover, Thelma’s newest boarder, looked after Leota and said, “So, I take it that when I need to see a doctor, I should make an appointment to see this Dr. Kerns?”

“Yes,” Annie, Deloris and Gracie said in unison.

Chapter Three

The Ship Dinner Club and Cocktail Lounge

Today was Friday. Her longest workday was because she worked both of her jobs—one in the morning at the switchboard and an evening shift at The Ship, where Deloris also worked on Saturdays. The Ship was one of the many cocktail lounges in Kansas City. She remembered when she got the job.

In September 1935, Deloris worked at the Log Tavern, a local hangout for the Young Democrats Club. It was also called the Prospect Inn located at 26th and Prospect. She lost the job there for slapping a committeeman. Neal Guardino, the owner, was pressured into firing Deloris. He told her he didn't want to fire her, but was being pressured by the committeeman.

Deloris had only worked at the Log Tavern for a few months when this happened. Neal felt badly for firing her and asked if she would like to work in a new cocktail lounge on 10th Street owned by a friend of his. When Neal asked her if she would like to work at The Ship, Deloris jumped at the chance. He said he would take her there because the job was only by referral. He stopped and asked, "You are twenty-one, aren't you?"

"I just turned twenty-three," was her reply. He then asked her if she was a registered voter, and she said, "Yes, and I vote, too!"

"I hope you voted the right way," he said with a wink.

"Absolutely!" she said triumphantly.

With Tom Pendergast controlling the city, she knew what he meant. She learned much later that Tom Pendergast wasn't exactly aboveboard with his business dealings and politics.

"If you don't mind my asking, what exactly happened with the councilman? I'd like your side of the story," Neal asked.

"He offered me a position on one of Mr. Pendergast's committees until I slugged him with my shoe for getting too fresh, causing him to wreck his car," she said with a slight groan as she rubbed her neck. "I injured my neck and back in the car wreck, but I'm doing better than he is. I heard his wife is divorcing him."

They laughed, and Neal said, "Well, he deserved it. I'm glad you're doing better now. I am certain everyone will be pleased with you."

That was music to Deloris's ears. She enjoyed working the nightclub circuit because she needed the social interaction to keep from getting bored, and she made good money from her tips. They especially helped her make ends meet. She kept the job at the switchboard for the same reason, but also to keep her up-to-date on crime happening in Kansas City, which fed her interest in mysteries.

The Ship Dinner Club and Cocktail Lounge, at 411 E. 10th Street, was an upscale nightclub set up exactly like a ship with nautical décor and featured the sound of waves crashing against a ship's hull. Because of its name and shipboard atmosphere, most of the clientele were sailors and marines. It had captain's chairs, barrels, ropes, an anchor in the window, and a picture of a lighthouse on the back wall. There were portholes for windows and even brass spittoons. On the main floor, in a back corner behind black curtains, was a hallway that led to the restrooms, or "head," as they were called in nautical terms. On the opposite side were the servers' dressing rooms and lockers. The kitchen where they cooked full chicken and steak dinners was at the very back. A balcony overlooking the main floor was accessed by climbing a winding staircase near the back. At the top of the stairs were three small rooms divided by walls that could fold and collapse to make one big room. The decorations outside the three rooms held hidden peepholes so you could look in to see what was happening.

Deloris met The Ship's new manager, Mark Corbane, and Neal told him about her run-in with the politician. He commended Deloris for standing up to him. "Good for you! You're hired, but you have to join the waitress union."

"No problem," she said, "I already belong to the union." She noticed that the waitresses' uniforms were more modest than at other places, but they were still a little short. "Momma wouldn't approve of them, either," she thought to herself. But Momma wasn't here to see her. It was a really good thing she didn't see her wearing the other uniforms at her previous jobs. Deloris smiled mischievously at that thought.

She learned a long time ago it wasn't what you know, but who you know in the Kansas City world of nightclubs, taverns, and supper clubs. She took a moment to reflect on her experiences working at the various nightclubs, taverns, and restaurants. She originally worked at the soda fountain at Poppy's Paradise Park when she moved to the city, but it and the amusement park closed at the end of the summer. Nino Binaggio, a silent partner at Poppy's Paradise Park, had hired her to work at the Venetian Gardens Italian Restaurant, owned and operated by his wife, Connie. When it was shot up by gangsters, her friend Stella helped her get a job at Stella's grandparents' restaurant, the Indiana Gardens Restaurant. While she enjoyed working at Indiana Gardens, she could make more money working fewer hours serving alcohol at other places in town after she turned twenty-one. Deloris still worked at Indiana Gardens to help on special occasions, though.

In the spring, she went back to work at Poppy's. When she turned twenty-one, she transitioned to work at the Beer Garden there; she needed a job through the winter again. One customer at the Beer Garden, Maurio Barberini, was a good friend of Nino Binaggio. Maurio offered her a job at the Outlander Tavern at 10th and Troost. She worked there for a few months when she was almost kidnapped. Maurio felt badly for putting her in that situation. He helped Deloris get a job at the Silver Slipper, located at 2625 Warwick Boulevard and owned by another of his friends, for her protection. The waitress uniforms at the Silver Slipper barely covered what the good Lord gave her, and it made her uncomfortable, but she needed the job.

One day, her former boss at the Venetian Gardens, Connie Binaggio, Nino's wife, came in with a group of friends to the Indiana Gardens Restaurant while she was working and recognized Deloris. Connie found out that Deloris was looking for more work in a place that had more modest outfits for the servers. Lucille, a friend of Connie's who owned Lucille's Paradise Club at 15th and Wabash, was with her. She offered Deloris a job on the spot, and Deloris worked there until it closed Christmas Eve 1933. Lucille then helped her get a job at the Log Cabin. But when she was fired from working there, Neal, the manager, asked her about working at The Ship. So, it did not surprise her she got this job through who she knew and not what she knew.

The following weekend, September 6,1935, she had started work at The Ship and found she really liked it. The best part was Mark Corbane, the manager, and Willie Long, the bartender. They were both decent men and always treated her with respect. That was hard to find in the tavern/bar world, especially when the waitresses had to wear such revealing uniforms. She even heard there were some nightclubs and lounges where the waitresses wore only see-through aprons—nothing else. She always made sure not to apply to those places. In many ways, the atmosphere at The Ship was different. It was lighthearted and jovial—a really fun but respectable place to work.

Mark only came in for a few hours each day and only came downstairs to make sure everything was running smoothly, which he knew he could trust Willie to do. His office was upstairs at the back of the establishment.

Willie was a jokester, but in a kindhearted way. Sometimes when Deloris came into work, she realized Willie had hidden all the pens and pencils in the place so that she couldn't use one and accidentally keep it. He had discovered that when any were missing, they always wound up in Deloris's possession, so he made her search for one before she could add it to her collection.

RayAnn was another server at The Ship. Deloris tolerated working with RayAnn, but had to watch her because she often found RayAnn borrowing Deloris's clothes without asking. If Deloris was delayed talking to a customer or cleaning up, and RayAnn cashed out before her, RayAnn would go into Deloris's locker and borrow whatever she wanted. Deloris's father made her a fox fur stole from some foxes he killed, and she found RayAnn wearing it out of The Ship one night. She went running after her and retrieved the stole, but strangely RayAnn saw nothing wrong with her taking the items. Deloris talked with her, and she seemed to understand, but was a little hurt that Deloris didn't share her clothing willingly. She thought of Deloris as a sister from whom she could borrow whenever she needed to. RayAnn did have some redeeming qualities, though. Whenever Deloris needed RayAnn to cover for her to take off from work, RayAnn did so without complaining.

Then there was the custodian, Junius C. Jones, who went by JC. As a man of color, he was treated like a second-class citizen, not to be seen up front around the bar. Deloris felt sorry for him. He spent his evenings hidden in the back room until there was a need for a clean-up, or he might be in the back alley having a smoke. Occasionally, he might even be involved in a game of dice in the alley. Deloris tried to check in with JC once or twice a night to bring him something to eat or drink.

On New Year's Eve that year, The Ship was really jumping. That was the night she met George Packard, who had the night off from working as a bellboy at the Pickwick Hotel and wandered into The Ship. Deloris had just broken up with Jimmy Giraldi, whom she had been dating for a while, when he got a really nice job opportunity to open and manage a new casino in Las Vegas. They had one last date that December, and then she met George. She was, however, also still dating Les Wells; a fellow she met at the Jameson Picnic in August 1931 when she solved a fourteen-year-old murder in Jameson.

Chapter Four

Suicide?

In her bedroom, Deloris smiled as she remembered Leota's chronic ailments and David's patience with her. He was so passionate about his patients, but when the research opportunity came about, he was very excited. He truly cared about treating people right. The prospect of what his research would mean to the future of prenatal care and patient treatments was now lost. Deloris ruminated not only on her loss, but on the extreme loss to humanity and what might have been.

A knock on her door brought Deloris back to reality. It was Gracie with the evening newspaper. The front-page headline in the afternoon paper read: "Suicide at the Pickwick Hotel." Deloris thanked Gracie, took the paper, and read where it was reported that Dr. Kerns had taken an excessive amount of arsenic poison. Her eyes filled with tears again, and she found it hard to continue. She shook her head and mumbled, "Poor David, what in the world happened to you between meeting me for lunch and the next morning?"

The newspaper reported that Dr. Kerns left a suicide note on the table that looked quickly scrawled on a sheet of paper. Buried in his briefcase were found two letters—one addressed to his mother and another to Deloris Markham. Even though Austin had told her about the note, she still didn't understand. The article continued, saying that Dr. Kerns was to meet Dr. Myron Cramer with James and James from New York City that evening. He checked into the Pickwick Hotel at about 6:00

p.m. on the evening of February 13th. Hotel security found his body at 7:00 a.m. the next day when Dr. Cramer insisted that something must be wrong when he failed to meet for breakfast. The paper labeled it an apparent suicide, and the investigating officers concurred because of the suicide note nearby. Even though Deloris knew Austin was going to investigate anyway, the statement angered her.

Suicide? No, Deloris didn't believe for one minute that he had committed suicide. She knew David, and she knew it wasn't true. And if it wasn't suicide, there was only one other option: murder. But who in the world would do this to him? Who didn't like David, the kindest, gentlest person she knew? Someone needed to get to the bottom of this and find out what really happened. Then and there, Deloris decided she knew David best. If no one besides Austin was going to look into his death, she was going to help Austin find out who murdered their dear friend.

Unable to sit and do-nothing Deloris gathered her purse and coat and went to the Pickwick Hotel. She didn't know what she was going to do when she got there, but she had to do something. When she arrived, she saw people bustling around the lobby, going about their lives oblivious to anything that had happened there the night before. Didn't they know this is where David breathed his last breath? It upset her to see them all going about their business as usual. Didn't they know the world lost a great man last night? Shouldn't there still be some police presence there? Some police tape, something? That's it! She entered the elevator. The elevator operator turned to her and asked, "Which floor, Miss?"

That's when she realized she didn't know what room David was staying in or even what floor to tell the young man.

"I, uh. I don't know." She froze, realizing that she should have asked her boyfriend, George Packard, a bellhop at the Pickwick Hotel, to find out what room David was in before coming there. Of course, he wasn't on duty yet, so he couldn't help her either. "Do you know what room Dr. David Kerns was staying in last night?"

"You mean the man who offed himself? I'm sorry, Miss, but I can't tell you that." The elevator was still on the lobby floor. He opened the cage door for her to exit, staring at her as she stepped out.

She stood in the lobby for about five minutes feeling helpless and vulnerable. She had never really felt that before and didn't know what to do or where to go. "What to do? What to do?" she thought to herself. Deloris slowly turned and exited the hotel. She would go home and try to figure things out before going to work her shift at The Ship.

Chapter Five

Valentine's Day

Valentine's Day 1936 was a miserable day. It was the worst Valentine's Day ever, and Deloris didn't feel like working anywhere. She needed to start her quest to find David's killer. Standing in her bedroom, Deloris squared her shoulders, and her violet eyes took on a hard glint. Her eyes had the same look when she had announced five years ago that she wasn't getting married and settling down in Jameson, but that she was moving to the big city to see the world. And now, here she was, living a life in the city. Her family might joke about her Irish stubbornness, but they also knew to be wary of that glint. When Deloris was determined, she meant business. This time, that inner hardness was shown for her friend. She would find David's murderer, and she would bring them to justice.

As she entered The Ship that night, she felt hollow inside, even though she found a bouquet of red roses and chocolates from Les and another box of chocolates and a card from George waiting for her at the bar. It was very sweet, but her heart wasn't in it. Deloris could have taken the night off to celebrate the Valentine's holiday—Mr. Corbane would have approved it—but Les was out of town and George couldn't take the night off, so she volunteered to work. She would also earn double time in pay working the holiday, but now she just couldn't muster any enthusiasm or joviality to flirt with the customers. Customers started coming in, and she took their orders. Her regulars brought her flowers, candy, and cards, too. When they saw her lack of enthusiasm, they asked what happened to her smile and what was wrong? She couldn't bring herself to answer. She fled to the dressing room a time or two, and Willie came from the bar to talk to her.

"I heard about your friend dying, and I know you are hurting," he said. Willie was always the voice of reason. "I'm sorry, kid. I know it is hard to go on, but sometimes we have to continue on, especially in this business. Your friend wouldn't want to see you hurting like this. The best thing for you to do right now is to keep busy, so you won't have time to think about it. Come on, Deloris, put on a stiff upper lip and try not to think about it right now. Besides, I need you out there to help me handle that ugly crowd of poor suckers without a date tonight. Don't make me face them alone," he smiled. "Remember RayAnn isn't here to help." Willie always knew what to say to make Deloris feel better. She managed a small smile and nodded her head.

"There she is. I knew you could do it," Willie said, giving her a brief, awkward hug before they both returned to the bar.

Later, Willie surprised Deloris with some cash. Apparently, he took up a small collection from the patrons in The Ship that night to help her with any expenses she might incur. That's when the tears really flowed.

The next day, Saturday, Deloris had already agreed to work the switchboard for Gracie because she didn't have plans. She regretted that now, too. She left for the switchboard early, skipping breakfast at home but snagging some cinnamon rolls from her favorite bakery, Wolferman's, along the way. When she arrived at the police station, a half-hour before she needed to clock in, she headed towards the big open room that housed the detectives' desks instead of going upstairs to the switchboard. She figured that Austin and his partner, Big

Jim Anderson, would be there on a Saturday morning working on David's case since they told her they weren't convinced it was a suicide either and they always seemed to work, even on weekends.

Joey Crabtree, a green-behind-the-ears new police recruit who only worked on weekends stopped her at the front desk. "Miss, you can't go back there! Not without being escorted," he said, holding up his hand.

"You can call me Deloris." She turned to face him and smiled sweetly. Then she flashed him very innocent-looking violet eyes. "Crabtree, is it?" she said as she looked at the name tag on his uniform. "What's your first name, Officer Crabtree?"

"Joey." He swallowed hard as he replied. He was mesmerized by this beautiful woman in front of him.

"Okay, Joey. You're new here, I understand, but look, I have to go back there. There's a letter I'm supposed to read from Dr. Kerns, the murder victim at the Pickwick Hotel. It was in the newspapers and everything. I work upstairs and go back there all the time."

"I'm sorry, Miss, but I can't let you through. Chief's orders."

She drew an exasperated breath. "Where are Detectives Martin and Anderson? They'll escort me back." Deloris stood on her tiptoes to look over the tall desk that was on a riser where Joey was seated and blocked the view into the back room, trying to find a familiar face who would wave her through.

"They're in a meeting with the chief." Joey finally noticed the bakery box in her arms. "Say, are those cinnamon rolls?"

Just then, she caught a glance into the back of the

detective's room where the door to Chief of Police Elden Douglas' office door opened. When Deloris saw Big Jim appear in the doorway still talking with Chief Douglas, she waved and called out.

"Yoo-hoo, Jim!"

Big Jim turned around and saw her waving. He yelled to Joey, "Let her through," and waved her back. Jim was well over six feet tall, with brown hair and turquoise green eyes. His height plus his former Marine training made him an intimidating figure who could give a suspect one look and they caved.

Deloris grinned at Joey and said, "Yes, they're cinnamon rolls, but not for you!" and she waltzed past him, holding the box out of his reach.

As she headed back to the detective's desk, she saw Rebecca Bradford, the sketch artist for the police department, sitting at another desk listening to a victim describe a suspect. Rebecca had helped her with a suspect drawing a year ago, and Deloris waved before continuing to Big Jim's desk.

"Hey, Jim, want a cinnamon roll? I would have offered one to the new guy at the front desk, but he wasn't nice to me." She winked and said this loudly enough for Joey to hear.

Big Jim smiled. "Sure. Coffee?"

"That'd be swell," Deloris responded.

As Jim got a spare coffee cup and walked over to the coffeepot which had just finished percolating, he gestured toward Austin, who was on the phone. "He should be done soon."

"I'll wait," she said, taking a seat at Big Jim's desk. "Do you have a small plate or something for these?"

"Sure. I'll grab some paper towels," he said as he handed her coffee.

"So, what can you tell me about this letter or the case?" Deloris asked.

Before Big Jim could respond, Austin ended his phone call and smiled when he turned and saw Deloris. "Hey, Short Stuff! How ya doin'?"

He walked over to her and uncharacteristically put an arm around her shoulders, looking down at her with concern.

"I've been better. Still can't believe David is gone." She took a white handkerchief with a pink scalloped edge and pink roses on it out of her purse and dabbed her eyes as a tear started a path down her cheek. She was touched by Austin's show of concern for her. He was apparently shaken up by David's death, too.

Austin nodded. "Yeah, we're looking into it." As Big Jim handed Deloris the paper towels, Austin asked, "Can you tell Big Jim about your lunch with David?"

Deloris nodded, took a big bite of cinnamon roll, a swig of coffee, and waited a moment before she talked.

"At this lunch, like all the others, we swapped stories, catching each other up on our respective lives. I started by telling him about my current boyfriends, and how unfortunately, they both had to work on Valentine's Day, leaving me a little annoyed. What's the point of having two boyfriends if they're not available to date?"

Austin interrupted, "Will you get to the point, please?"

"Okay, okay. Well, he told me about his frustrations with his mother, but he was also concerned because she had been having health issues lately and wouldn't let him run tests. So, he was going to the library to look some things up to see if he could find medicine to help her or to figure out what was making her sick."

"Go on," Big Jim urged.

"Well, then he started telling me about his research with the famous doctor from New York, and I told him I had just received my copy of the Jameson newspaper that my mother sends me every week and there was an article about it. I then asked him about the Blue Mass, and he told me it was when Bert, my oldest brother Roy's wife, died four years ago that first made him interested in researching the potential dangers of Blue Mass."

Choked up, Deloris looked down and paused before filling Big Jim in on Bert's and her babies' deaths.

"Back when we — Austin and I — lived in Jameson, my sister-in-law, Bert Markham, had been sick during pregnancy. She took Blue Mass regularly, and when the twin baby boys were born, one was stillborn and the other one died a day later. Bert died just a few days after that, and the autopsy revealed it was from a combination of septicemia and mercury poisoning. The key ingredient in Blue Mass is mercury." Austin stood there, nodding his head in agreement and gave Deloris a pat on the shoulder.

"When Bert died along with the twin baby boys, everyone in Jameson grieved, and my brother was totally devastated. David was a close friend of my brother and Bert, and her death hit him pretty hard as well. I always suspected that he had a little crush on her." She sighed. "Anyway, he vowed to learn more about the dangers of Blue Mass, but he hadn't completed his medical training at that time, so once he started his practice, he began researching it." She looked up at Austin and added, "I don't remember if I told you that his research led to the opportunity to go to work with Dr. Myron Cramer."

"Yes, you already told me about the research on the phone, but you were pretty distraught," Austin said.

"Oh yes," Deloris remembered. "Well, he cut our lunch short because he was headed to the library before meeting with Dr. Cramer whom he was excited to meet."

As she finished telling Austin and Big Jim about her lunch with David, she sniffled, and Austin gave her his plain white handkerchief, saying, "We're going to sort this out, Deloris."

"Oh, I have my handkerchief here. Thank you," she replied as she pulled it out of her sleeve and dabbed her eyes. Recovering her composure, she said, "You'd better find out who did this to David. I'm going to help you."

"Sure, kid," Big Jim consoled. He knew that once she said she was going to help, there was no use talking her out of it. Besides, she had been a great help in solving past murders.

Deloris straightened in her chair. "Now, where is this letter you told me about?" she asked.

Austin nodded at Big Jim as he said, "Jim, can you take Deloris over to the evidence room? I need to make a call."

Big Jim stood up and gently said, "Follow me, please."

"Let us know what you make of the letter, okay?" Austin asked as he turned toward the phone.

"Absolutely," Deloris said as she checked the time on her wristwatch. She realized that she'd better read quickly or she would be late for her shift. Jim introduced her to the officer on duty in the evidence room.

The evidence officer told her she could look at the letter but needed to return it until the death was officially ruled a suicide. She asked if she could read it in private and return it momentarily. With his approval, she took it into the ladies' restroom to read it, grabbing a pad of paper and a pen from a desk as she walked by. Propping the pad on her purse, she took notes as she read.

Neatly written on the envelope were the words:

In the event of my death, please give
this letter to Deloris Markham.

It was unusual for a doctor to have neat penmanship, and perhaps that is why he printed it to make it more easily read. Miss Tennison, their high school penmanship teacher, would be so proud of him, but David was an exceptional man in many ways.

Chapter Six

The Letter

Because the ladies' room at the police station was small with three stalls, Deloris barred the door by propping a mop handle against it to prevent anyone walking in on her. There was one old, dirty wingback chair in the room that looked like it came out of a trash heap. It even had a wire sticking up from the seat. Rather than sitting on it normally, she pulled the plain white handkerchief she always carried out of her purse and put it down on the arm of the chair. She sat gingerly on the armrest with her back leaning against the back of the chair and the wall. Taking a deep breath, she opened the sealed envelope with her fingernails.

The contents of David's letter read:

Hello DeDe,

If you are reading this, then I must be dead. I know that my death must have come as a shock to you, and I am very sorry, but the circumstances are out of my control. Do you remember when we met at the after-school picnic on the banks of the Grand River and I told you how much I loved you? That was the happiest day of my life. And then I kissed you behind the fire escape at school when we returned from the picnic? I wish we could go back to those simpler times. Time passes much too quickly now and, like the sand in an hourglass, it slips through our fingers.

Please remember me fondly and tell your brother Allen, the detective, to go have a beer on me.

With warmest regards and all my love,

Dr. David Kerns

Deloris quickly copied the letter on her pad of paper, but she was beyond confused. Why was David writing to her about how much their relationship meant to him and then saying things that, at face value, didn't make any sense? Slowly, she realized the letter was in code. He was obviously afraid of the information he'd written falling into the wrong hands.

But what information was that? Deloris reread the letter for clues, taking notes and underlining what was curious or odd. First, David never called her DeDe; only Deloris's closest friends, family, and high school classmates called her that. It was a name she was given in grade school because she had a bad stutter, and when asked her name, all she could say was DeDe. David normally called her Deloris, so that was a little strange.

Second, he didn't attend her senior class end-of-school picnic. The school picnic was only for her class and held on the banks of the Grand River on a very rainy, muddy day. David had already graduated several years before, and he certainly never told her he loved her. They never had that kind of relationship, so there must be a clue there. He also never kissed her behind the fire escape, or anywhere else, for that matter, so that must be another clue.

"'Go back to simpler times'" means he wants me to go back to the fire escape, maybe?" she mused. She flipped the pad of paper to a new page and started making a list: DeDe, school picnic at Grand River, kiss behind the fire escape at the

Jameson School, hourglass, and Allen.

“Now, what does the hourglass and sand slipping through fingers mean?” she wondered. “It must be a clue, but sand in an hourglass can’t slip through one’s fingers. It is contained. Hourglass must be a clue to something, but what? Is it simpler times?”

Next, she didn’t have a brother named, Allen. Did he mean Austin? Austin was like her brother because they grew up together, but he was a good friend, and David knew that. But Austin was a detective. Deloris smiled. She was pretty sure she had this clue figured out—David wanted her to talk to and work with Austin to solve his puzzles.

Finally, she looked at the signature. “Who signs a love letter, Dr. David Kerns?” she asked the empty restroom. Shouldn’t he have signed it ‘Love, Dave or David’ to show familiarity? Was this supposed to be because he wanted her to remember that he was a doctor? She didn’t think that was much of a clue.

The bathroom door rattled as someone tried to enter. Deloris called out, “Occupied!” then went back to deciphering.

The door rattled again, and a voice on the other side said, “All three stools can’t be occupied, can they? Why did you lock the door?”

“Still occupied! Sorry! I’ll be out in a minute,” Deloris called out and then went back to her notes.

The hourglass really had her puzzled. What or where was an hourglass? If it wasn’t a clue, why did he say it that way?

The door rattled again. “C’mon, open up!” Deloris realized it was Rebecca, the sketch artist.

Deloris hopped up, jammed the papers into her purse,

flushed the toilet, and removed the mop so the door could open. Rebecca burst in and gave her a dirty look.

"Sorry," Deloris apologized, then left the restroom.

She checked her watch and realized that she didn't have much time left before she needed to return the letter and start her shift at the switchboard. Deloris decided she would try to decipher more of the letter later. "What was in Mrs. Kerns's letter?" she wondered. Maybe it would explain the hourglass.

Instead of handing the letter back to the evidence officer, she walked straight past his desk, looking for Austin and Big Jim.

"Miss!" the officer called out. "Miss, you'll have to return the letter!"

"Don't be a wet sock," Deloris tossed over her shoulder. "I have to find the detectives!"

Keeping his eye on the letter in Deloris's hand, the officer followed her back to the detectives' offices. This time Joey didn't stop her. Luckily, Austin was still there.

"Austin, this letter—it's got to be a clue." Deloris announced, waving the letter wildly in the air.

The evidence officer winced. "Miss, could you please be careful with the evidence?"

Deloris ignored him. "It's written like a love letter, but we were never in love, and he talks about things that never happened," she said

Austin was shocked. "Are you sure, DeDe?"

"There! That is one clue. He never called me DeDe. I am positive this whole letter is filled with clues," she replied.

Austin took the letter, much to the evidence officer's relief, and read it over carefully as Deloris explained her theory. When she was done, he looked somber.

"Thanks, DeDe. Let's go talk to the chief."

Austin, carrying the letter, walked over to Chief Douglas' door. Deloris followed him, with the evidence officer trailing along behind. He was obviously still trying to figure out a way to get the letter back into his possession.

Austin handed the chief the letter, told him about the strange message, and explained Deloris's theory that the letter was actually full of clues.

"But why write it?" the Chief Elden Douglas asked, staring at the letter. "Did he know something was going to happen?"

Austin shook his head. "I don't know, Chief. But I want to investigate. I really don't believe this was a suicide."

There was a knock on the door, and a woman wearing a lab coat stuck her head in. Carolyn Bechtel, the assistant coroner, an attractive woman with short brown hair and soft brown eyes, opened by saying, "Chief Douglas, here's the coroner's report you asked for." She glanced at Austin and gave a small nod, followed by a shy smile.

"Come on in," the Chief replied. "We were just talking about the victim. What did you find out, Miss Bechtel?"

"Yes, what did you find out?" Deloris asked eagerly.

Carolyn looked at the Chief, who nodded his head and said, "She'll find out one way or another, so you may as well include her."

"I found," Carolyn paused slightly. "Dr. David Kerns took an excessive amount of poison, but the bottle of Blue Mass that was found next to his bed was not what killed him. The cause of death was a lethal dose of arsenic, although he had a large dose of mercury in his system too."

The combination of the letter and the coroner's report convinced Chief Douglas. Austin handed the letter back to the evidence officer, who was more than happy to retrieve possession of it finally. The chief turned to Austin and said, "Go ahead. You can officially open up an investigation into Dr. David Kerns's death."

"Right," Austin said, and then he glanced at his watch. "DeDe, aren't you working today? Don't you have to get upstairs?" Deloris gasped and rushed out.

Once seated at the switchboard, Deloris was eager to get through her work so that she could continue trying to make some sense of David's letter. The two clues she was most sure about were the school picnic and the fire escape. It would make sense if David had left her something in Jameson, since they both knew the town well. She'd let Austin and Big Jim do the investigating in Kansas City, for now, while she would go up home and follow the clues there. She was eager to look around the fire escape.

When she got home that afternoon, she learned Leota had stayed home in her room sick that day. She hoped she wouldn't catch what she had. There was too much for her to do to be sick.

Deloris started making preparations to clear her calendar to take some days off so that she could go to Jameson and begin her own investigation. She didn't work the next day, Sunday, and had some time off coming at the switchboard, so it shouldn't be too hard to find someone to cover the Monday and Tuesday morning shifts for her. Three days off should help her figure something out. She would ask Gracie or one of the women who worked the afternoon, evening, or weekend shifts to work Monday and Tuesday mornings for her. She had to work that night at The Ship. Then she wouldn't need to come back until next Friday night, so she had six days off from it. Everything was falling into place. Tomorrow, she would begin following the clues from David's letter, but tonight, she had a shift at The Ship.

When Deloris got to The Ship, Mark Corbane called her over to a table. There was only one customer in the bar, and Willie was talking to him, so it was semi-private. Mr. Corbane handed Deloris a handful of money. He explained that a customer from the night before had felt sorry for her and brought it by earlier that afternoon. Deloris quickly stuck it in her bra, which she called her secret pocket. It, plus the money Willie gave her last night, would help her pay for the bus tickets and any taxi rides she would need to take in her investigation. On her break, she found a used envelope to write a list of what she needed to do before going up home—pack, get a ride to the bus station, etc.

Right now, she could use that pad of paper from the detective's desk she had borrowed earlier, but Austin retrieved it from her before she left. Paper was still a little scarce since the Great Depression, so she often "borrowed" paper from her workstation at the switchboard. Well, actually, she often found pads of paper and several pens and pencils that had accidentally wound up in her purse when she got home from work. She didn't intend to steal them; she just accidentally forgot to return them. But this time she had returned most of them and had forgotten to leave one pad of paper and a pen or two in her purse. She hoped she still had a pad of paper and a pen or pencil stashed away in her room so she could take them with her to write on when she discovered something related to the case in Jameson.

For now, two customers walked in and took a seat, and she needed to get their orders. "What can I get for you? Two beers, a Kansas City strip steak and a sirloin. How would you like them fixed? Okay, the KC strip rare and the sirloin well done. Baked potato okay with that? Got it. Coming right up."

Back home that night, she barely got any sleep. When she tried to close her eyes, she thought of David. It didn't help that she could hear Leota sobbing and crying in her bedroom upstairs. Her room was directly above Deloris's room. Then she heard her run across the floor and down the stairs to the bathroom, where she was sick.

Deloris knocked on the bathroom door. "Are you all right in there? Can I get you anything?" She would have offered her a shoulder to cry on even, but Leota yelled, "Go away!" and Deloris understood. She wasn't certain that she could help Leota through her own grief when she was having trouble helping herself. She finally managed a few hours of sleep, with a busy day ahead.

Chapter Seven

Jameson

Morning came, and Deloris found herself wide awake, unlike on a normal Sunday morning when she liked to sleep in, but she was eager to get started digging for facts. The first stop was to catch the earliest bus heading north to Jameson. Yesterday, on her break, she rang up her mother to tell her she was coming home for a couple of days. She didn't tell her about David because she wanted to tell her in person. She knew the newspaper in her small town wouldn't know about his death yet, and only she and Thelma knew about him. Mrs. Kerns didn't socialize with her mother or anyone else in the town anymore. She had moved on. Deloris was relatively certain that neither her mother nor anyone else in Jameson would know David had been murdered yet.

Her mother and father, Nannie and Will Markham, would be glad to see her and Clarence, her older brother, who would pick her up at the bus stop in Pattonsburg. Her oldest brother, Roy, lived nearby, and she hoped to see him as well, to tell him about his friend's death in person. After Bert's death, Roy had gone to work on the Hoover Dam for a few years until Momma called him to come home and help with the farm. That year was a bumper crop of beans, and it was a call for all hands-on deck to get them harvested before they dried up and rotted on the vine. He stayed afterward and bought a small farm north of Gallatin, less than ten miles south of his parents' farm.

After Sunday dinner and a brief visit, she would ask Clarence if he would take her to the schoolhouse and on Monday to the banks of the Grand River. Deloris didn't drive, but usually she could find someone to give her a ride. If neither he nor Roy could take her, then she would hitch up the team of horses to the buck wagon and go there and wherever else the clues might take her if it was close by.

She brought a canvas bag with her to collect whatever she might find. The bag also became her emergency kit. Besides a flashlight, rope, and a small baseball bat for protection, she had various other items to use in case of an emergency. She also needed to remember to bring the pad of paper she "found from the switchboard" in her bedroom last night, along with a couple of pencils and a pocket knife to sharpen the pencils. She looked at the notes she had made on the envelope and rewrote a more organized plan of her to-dos on the pad of paper. Her first stop would be the fire escape at the Jameson R-3 School building to look around, inside and behind it, because there shouldn't be any students there on a Sunday afternoon.

As the blue and white Greyhound bus neared the Pattonsburg bus stop, Deloris could see Clarence with his hat cocked to one side, smoking a cigarette with one foot on the running board of his Model A. He threw his cigarette down and stomped on it to put it out before he started walking to the bus stop, giving Deloris a short wave as it passed. Before Deloris stepped off the bus, she handed Clarence her small suitcase, keeping her emergency bag over her right shoulder. With his other hand, Clarence took her hand and held it as she jumped down from the bottom step. She could tell he was happy to see her, but wouldn't hug her because it wouldn't be proper.

On the seven-mile journey home from the bus stop, she

told him about David, the reported suicide, and the letter. He was angry at first and then intrigued by the scavenger hunt. He readily agreed to take her around when his chores were finished. Clarence remembered David from school, but David was four years older. Clarence quit school after eighth grade because he was needed to work on the farm. At fourteen, he also went to work for David's father at the popcorn factory for a few years until Mr. Kerns died from a heart attack. The popcorn factory burned down shortly thereafter. He liked Mr. Kerns as a boss and was eager to help Deloris find out who killed his son, if he had been murdered.

Normally, several family members came home for Sunday dinner, but on this day only her brother Roy showed up because of the heavy snow in the other parts of northern Missouri where other family members lived. Roy always came home for Sunday dinner and often through the week for some of his momma's home cooking.

Roy and David had been in the same class at school. With only three boys in the class, they all became fast friends. When Deloris told Roy about David, his face went from sorrow to anger.

"If Clarence can't take you around, I'll drive over here and get you," Roy said, his eyes hard with an uncharacteristic look of fury in them and fists clenched.

Clarence assured Roy, "I've got it taken care of, brother. I shouldn't have any problems getting my chores done and taking her around to follow the clues. Besides, I worked for David's father, and I want to help and see the person who did this arrested."

"Thank you both. All I need to do is get my canvas bag, and I will be ready to go after we eat," Deloris said with gratitude.

After a hearty Sunday dinner at noon, Deloris and Clarence left for the schoolyard to see what they could find. The snow was melting in this area, and the roads were muddy, but the narrow tires on the Model A managed to cut through the mire as Clarence maneuvered the car from side to side to find solid ground. Excited about what she might find around or behind the fire escape, she talked Clarence's ear off as he drove.

Pulling up to the three-story red brick school building, Deloris and Clarence exited the car and walked to the east side of the building where the fire escape stood. It was a long metal tube, strapped and secured to the building with metal ties bolted into the brick, that started at the third floor and went all the way to two feet above the ground at the bottom. They figured whatever they would find would not be inside the tube because it could easily be dislodged if the students came down the fire escape, so they searched around it. They looked under rocks and at the bricks on the building to see if any of them were loose. Nothing. Then, on the back of the tube towards the bottom, Deloris saw something. She could see a partial number painted on the tube. She pushed snow and ice aside to look at it. There she saw a series of numbers: L4 56 R3 47 L2 89. What in the world? She wasn't sure if that was a clue or not, but she saw nothing else. Either the clue was gone, or this was it. She pulled a pencil and a pad of paper out of her bag and wrote the numbers down and where they were found. After one last look around, Clarence said they should go home.

As the sun gradually fell below the horizon on their way home, they discussed what the numbers could mean. They followed the lonely country lane, embraced by a line of trees, up to the house. In the summer, the trees provided a canopy from the brutal sun, but today they were nothing but bare limbs. When the house came into view, it looked like a

Currier and Ives print, with the kerosene lamps giving off a warm golden glow through the windows. The barn was barely visible, with its large black outline against the darkening sky. Rural electricity hadn't come to this part of the country yet. Inside the kitchen, Deloris sat at the table, telling her parents what she had found.

"I don't like you traipsing around chasing another murderer, and I'm not happy that you dragged Clarence into it. It's unladylike, and I won't have any daughter of mine running around acting like a hooligan!" Nannie unleashed her displeasure.

Deloris's father sat there quietly, listening to what she had to say, then in a calm, soothing voice said, "Now Nannie, let's hear her out on this. You said you found a combination of numbers?

Deloris repeated the numbers, "L4 56 R3 47 L2 89."

Then, he offered a suggestion that made perfect sense. "Could they be the combination to a safe? That's what they sound like to me."

"A safe?" Deloris looked at the numbers again, and suddenly they made sense. "Yes, a safe. But where is this safe that we need to open," Deloris asked.

"I guess that's what you need to find out," her father said.

"There's also an hourglass," Deloris added. "Where do you think we will find an hourglass?"

"I have no idea," her father answered as he got and walked to the coffeepot. Nannie was glaring at him throughout this conversation, and he avoided looking at her as he walked past her.

Upstairs in Deloris's bedroom, she reflected upon the clues and conversation with her father. What mystery could the safe and the hourglass hold? She would worry about them later. For now, she needed to get some sleep for the busy day ahead, as the day's activities suddenly caught up with her.

Monday morning after chores, Clarence drove Deloris over the Lewis Mill Bridge, a covered metal truss bridge, on the banks of the Grand River. About a quarter of a mile from the spot where the graduation picnic had been held several years before, Clarence pulled off the road. It was impossible to get any closer through the cornfield because of the mud and a large puddle in the middle of the path. Every year the graduating class had a picnic there, so everyone knew its location.

Exiting the car, Deloris was bundled up with so many layers of clothes that she could barely move. Luckily, the old boots that she had left at her parents were still there, ready for her to wear today. She grabbed a sturdy stick that she found nearby to help keep her balance. They walked the distance across the field to the bank of the river. Deloris almost lost a boot in the mucky, gunky mire when she stepped in the mud and the suction started pulling it off her foot. But because she was expecting it to happen — it had happened to her before— she was prepared. She stopped before her foot came out of the boot and she stepped into the thick, cold mud. Clarence came over to help her keep her balance as she dropped the stick not too far in front of her, so that she could hold on to him. Pulling the top of the boot up with one hand and holding on to Clarence's arm with the other, she eventually pulled it out of the mud with her foot still inside. Laughing at the memories of past instances when she came home with a muddy foot, she picked up the walking stick, and they continued on towards the river.

When they reached the riverbank, she and Clarence searched around the trees, under snow, rocks, and the heavy blanket of fallen leaves. Deloris used the stick to poke around a fire site left by someone who had obviously been there just a few months before them. Then she poked around in the patches of snow, jabbing them here and there, hoping to hit something solid. About three feet down the bank from the fire's ashes, Clarence found a fallen, hollow tree and shined his flashlight to look inside. He thought he saw something and called Deloris over. He took the stick and poked it into the tree, pushing dead leaves aside as Deloris held the flashlight beam on the object. About three feet deep inside the log there appeared a small, round metal chewing tobacco box. Clarence used the stick to drag the box close enough that Deloris could reach in to grab it. She lifted the lid to reveal a safe deposit box key numbered 73 and a small piece of paper that had the initials JFB on it. She handed the box to Clarence to inspect.

"JFB, do you think this is a key to a safe deposit box at the Jameson Farmer's Bank?" she asked.

"There's only one way to find out," Clarence said with a proud smile because he found the key.

With the box in hand, she and Clarence made plans to go to the bank later that afternoon once they cleaned up.

At home, Deloris took her boots off on the back porch and walked into the kitchen in her stocking feet. Clarence took his boots off and put on another pair he had on the porch before entering the kitchen. Her mother said, "There you two are. Where'd you git to?"

"Oh, Clarence took me to look at Grand River," she replied modestly. "We're going to get cleaned up and go to the bank in town. We think we found a key to a safe deposit box, possibly David's."

"I know'd you two were up ta sumthin. At least be careful. While you're there, git me some flour, will ya?"

"We will, Momma," Deloris said and ran up the stairs before Momma could ask more questions. Given how upset she was last night, Deloris didn't like to lie to her, but she felt it was necessary. She preferred to omit the whole truth.

On the five-mile route to the bank, Clarence and Deloris each guessed what they might find if the key was to a safe deposit box there. Thankfully, the country roads to Highway 13 were drying out a little and were not as snowy or muddy as they had been earlier. The winter sun almost had the snow cleared on Highway 13, too.

Clarence reminded Deloris, "When we get there, don't dilly-dally around. Remember, we need to hurry before the bank closes so we won't need to come back the next morning. "Oh, and don't let me forget to get the flour."

Deloris agreed and added that she needed to catch the bus back to Kansas City the next morning, if possible. If the key didn't fit a security box at this bank, then Deloris would need to wait until her next time off to come back up home and try another bank. Perhaps if the key didn't work at the Jameson bank, maybe it would fit a safe deposit box at the Coffey, Pattonsburg, or one of the Gallatin banks. Of course, it might even be to a bank in the city, but Deloris hoped that wouldn't be the case.

Clarence pulled his car into the diagonal parking space in

front of the bank and turned the key to the car's ignition off. Deloris and Clarence entered the Jameson Farmer's Bank, and Clarence took a seat in the lobby. Deloris walked to the teller cage, where she saw a former classmate, Dorothy Braxton, standing inside. Dorothy worked at the bank while she was in high school and continued working there after she graduated. Noting a name change on Dorothy's nameplate, Deloris remembered hearing that she got married recently.

Deloris told Dorothy that David Kerns wanted her to retrieve something from his safe deposit box while she was in Jameson and bring it back to him in the city. She was banking on Dorothy having not heard the news of his death yet, and she was right. Dorothy looked through the Rolodex of cards until she stopped at one and produced a signature card; Deloris saw David had signed the card just the week before. "Bingo," she thought to herself with a smile. Deloris signed her name on the signature card and then his on the same line, and Dorothy replaced it in the Rolodex.

Deloris followed Dorothy to the room behind the teller cages that had a wall of two hundred metal boxes decorated with gold filigree scrolls around the edges of each box and numbers hammered into their front in the same gold filigree. Each box had two keyholes. Dorothy grabbed the ring of keys from the nail on the wall outside the room and found the one with a 73 on it that matched the key Deloris had in her hand. Near the bottom of the boxes, Deloris saw one with the number 73 and pointed it out to Dorothy.

"I see it!" Dorothy responded in a slightly agitated tone.

She plugged the key into the slot and took the key from Deloris to do the same in the other keyhole. She turned both keys simultaneously and, to Deloris's relief, the key worked.

Opening the outer door, Dorothy pulled the long metal box from its resting place and handed it to Deloris.

Walking into another smaller room used for customers to go through their safety deposit boxes privately, Deloris closed the door and sat down at the small wooden table, placing the box in the middle. Excited and yet apprehensive about what she would find, she lifted the metal lid and peered in. Several official-looking papers were in there along with some money, and a pocket watch with a note attached to it that identified it as belonging to David's father. There was also what looked like a house key. She figured he must want her to go to his house. She also found the deed to his house, plus an envelope addressed to his lawyer. In the back of the safe deposit box were several jeweled men's cufflinks, a man's wristwatch, and a ring box. Deloris picked up the small box and opened it slowly to reveal a truly exquisite diamond ring. "This must be the ring David planned to use to propose to Lucy McCoy," Deloris thought. He never did after he caught her cheating on him with Bob Scott. David told Deloris all about Lucy and Bob when he pointed them out to her when he saw them across the street one evening.

Running her hand around the inside of the safe deposit box, Deloris found nothing else that might be a clue, so she scooped the entire contents out and put them into her canvas bag. She wrapped all the jewelry in her handkerchief and tucked it into a corner of the bag. She had a plan for the pocket watch and put it in her purse instead.

Time was not on her side to examine each paper here, so she decided she would look at them when she returned to her parents' house. Handing the empty box back to Dorothy when she exited the room, she and Clarence left the bank. They walked the short distance to the grocery store and bought the flour for Momma. (Little did she know that just a few short months later, her beloved Jameson and its Main Street would be ravaged by a major fire, and the bank would be no more. When that happened, she was doubly glad that she had cleaned out that safe deposit box.)

Daylight was waning, and the sky looked threatening, and Clarence reminded Deloris that they had better head back home before it became too dark. Deloris agreed, and they talked up a storm, excited about their find. Deloris opened the bag and removed the chewing tobacco box. She replaced the safe deposit box key and put in the house key as well. When they arrived home, Deloris emptied the bag onto the kitchen table to examine everything. "Deloris, whaddaya have there?" Her mother asked as she walked into the kitchen from the back porch.

Before Deloris answered her question, she looked at Clarence and then up at her momma sheepishly.

"I uh-uh," Deloris stuttered.

"I know'd you been running around doin this detecting stuff anyway. People saw you and Clarence acting suspicious like. But then I figured it t'was fer Mrs. Kerns so go ahead and tell me what you been up to."

"We found the key to David's safe deposit box and discovered it fit a box at the bank in town!" Deloris answered excitedly. "I brought all the items from the box home, and we want to look at them here." Deloris nodded to Clarence to include him, and he nodded back.

"I don't feel comfortable going through David's personal papers, and no one else except Deloris, whom he entrusted his secrets to, should look at them, either," Momma said with a stern look at Clarence. "Besides, I need her to clean off the table and help me get supper on the table."

Embarrassed, Clarence shrank back from the table and said, "Yes, Momma."

Deloris understood and reluctantly put everything back in her bag with plans to review the papers as soon as she returned to the security of her bedroom in the city. She wondered if her secret hiding place at Thelma's would hold the bag and its contents. She put the bag at the foot of the stairs and returned to help her mother with the meal.

Roy came over to join them for supper, and the conversation around the table that night was electric. Deloris and Clarence told of their escapades searching the school grounds, and then Clarence told about their going to the banks of the Grand River, and about Deloris almost losing her boot. Everyone had a big laugh over it and related that it had happened to each of them. Their father offered words of encouragement to them and said how he was sure Blanche Kerns would be happy they found these items for her. It made Deloris feel good to have her father's blessing, and she thought she saw her mother nod at his statement.

Roy was curious to know what she would find in the papers. "You'll let me know if there are any more clues in those papers? And definitely let me know who murdered David. It makes me so angry. I want to help you."

"I'll let you know what I find out. Don't worry, we'll find out who did this and put them away for a very long time," Deloris consoled her big brother.

Upstairs in her bed, she realized it was getting too late, and she needed to get up early the next morning. She was disappointed, but Deloris figured she would have plenty of time to go through everything at Thelma's. So, she quickly packed all of her things and put the bags at the foot of her bed, but not before laying out an outfit to wear tomorrow on the bus. She drifted off to sleep quickly.

Chapter Eight
More Clues

Deloris was up early Tuesday morning, ready to leave. Her parents rode with her and Clarence to the bus stop to catch the eight o'clock bus to Kansas City. After saying her goodbyes, she boarded the bus and took a seat next to the window so that she could wave at them as it pulled out. Her overnight bag fit perfectly in the overhead bin. She clutched the canvas tightly on her lap, afraid of losing it. She'd be back in Kansas City by eleven after several stops along the way, and the taxi would have her home by eleven-thirty, leaving plenty of time that afternoon to examine everything she'd found in Jameson. Then she would plan her next step.

Once back at home and safe in her room, Deloris removed the papers and read each one carefully. There were stock certificates dating back to the late 1880s that looked as if they were worth a fortune. Another document was the Last Will and Testament of Mr. Zebediah Kerns, David's father. She even found David's birth certificate, signed by old Doc Graham. She didn't know his middle name was Edward—David Edward Kerns. David's diploma from the university for his bachelor's degree was there; she remembered seeing his medical school diploma on the wall in his office. The final document was a copy of David's mother's Last Will and Testament, dated five years ago, when she left all her worldly belongings to David after his father's death.

Deloris discovered years ago that two of the wooden

floorboards under her bed were loose. When she pried them up, they provided the perfect hiding spot — a space about a foot and a half deep and twelve inches wide between the floor joists. It was Deloris's secret hiding spot for love letters from her boyfriends, her diary, and the few pieces of good jewelry that she owned and didn't wear very often. She pushed her bed over, moved the hand-knotted rug that covered the floorboards, and pried the boards up with a screwdriver that she kept in her canvas bag. Her love letters, diary, and jewelry were placed inside the canvas bag, too. Thankfully, the canvas bag fit perfectly, though snugly, between the floor joists—she worried it wouldn't. Returning the boards and the wrought-iron bed to their original positions, Deloris then threw the rug down on the floor beside her bed. The rug covered about half of the slats, so that the edges facing out from that side of the bed were covered.

Deloris sat for a few minutes in her room, thinking and planning, until Thelma knocked on her door and said that lunch was ready. Deloris called out, "Down in a minute." She quickly finished writing some notes, then went downstairs for lunch. Glancing around the room, she was surprised to see so many there for lunch on a weekday and dressed up so nicely.

Thelma sat at the head of the table with her daughters, the neighbor girls Evie and Nora Davis, and Gracie Burnett to her right, and Annie, Deloris, and Leota to her left. Cecilia sat at the other end of the table.

When Thelma divorced the girls' father, her in-laws helped her buy the boardinghouse. They were embarrassed at their son's misadventures and did it to provide a means of support for Thelma and the girls. She only rented rooms to single females and didn't allow male guests after ten o'clock. To supplement her income, Thelma also worked at the local egg factory through the week and as a lunch cook at a small cafe on weekends.

Thelma's caring nature led people to mistakenly believe they could take advantage of her, but she lived through some hard times and wasn't a pushover. She was a no-nonsense type of person, just like her mother. People also learned that when you mess with her family—watch out. She had recently cut her red hair to make it easier to take care of and shorten her time getting ready, although she still took the time to put her hair up in pin curls at night and wore a nightcap to protect them. Thelma regularly wore practical dresses covered with a full apron to protect them from cooking and chores.

Evelyn "Evie" Davis and her younger sister Nora lived next door with her parents, Ben and Charlotte Davis. She regularly wore the latest styles with a hat cocked to one side and her hair pinned up.

Evie was wearing a long-sleeved, two-tone sage and cream cotton sailor dress with a cinched belt. Her cream and light brown oxford-style shoes laced up and had a two-inch heel. Her hair was pulled back into a business-style bun. She knew she looked cute in her matching attire, and it showed on her face. Evie had a way of lighting up a room with her enthusiasm and curiosity. Her light blue-gray doe-eyes sparkled with the chance to be included at Thelma's table and hear about Deloris's adventures.

Lenora "Nora" Davis wore a navy-blue shirtwaist dress with a white collar that was indicative of high school attire.

Gracie's apparel matched her mood and her eyes. She wore a green mid-calf dress topped with a cropped top and brown leather slip-on pumps. A decorative bow topped her shoes.

Annie Bailey sat to Thelma's left. She wore her typical style of apparel: a tweed business suit with a blouse that tied at the neck. Her shoes were black Oxford style, adding to her business attire. She tried to control her curly hair and put it in a bun, but it escaped as it often did, no matter her efforts, so she pinned it with numerous hairpins. Her azure-blue eyes complemented her strawberry-blonde hair.

Deloris sat next to Annie and smoothed the wrinkles from her deep purple, flowered frock with her hands. Her medium-brown Mary Jane-type shoes with a small heel were brand new and slightly pinched her feet. A strand of her brown, medium-length hair fell into her violet eyes, and she brushed it back with her hand. When it fell again, she moved the hairpin closer to pin the strand back from her face. She felt the dress enhanced her violet eyes, and from the approving nod from Evie, she felt she had accomplished the look.

Leota Jones sat on Deloris's other side. Her brown eyes were often focused on the floor or away from other people, and today was no exception. Her clothes often looked frumpy, with dark browns and gray colors she covered with a full flowered apron like Thelma's. Deloris understood why she didn't dress up because taking care of the girls wasn't a glamorous job where you wear your finest clothes. You save them for something special, but even when she had something special, she didn't wear bright colors.

Leota typically sat on the other side of the table with Thelma's daughters, but because Evie was sitting there, she sat on the side with Annie and Deloris. Thelma's daughters were off from school because of a mumps outbreak in their class. They weren't sick, but it was precautionary.

Cecilia sat at the other end of the table from Thelma.

Cecilia's style of clothes today was more casual with her pastel blue Nelly Don style cotton shirtwaist mid-calf length dress.

Thelma commented, "It is nice having everyone home during a workday for lunch, and today I invited Evie and Nora to join us since their parents are out of town and I understand Nora had a day off from school. Evie, you said that your schedule has you out of school on Tuesday afternoons, correct?"

"Yes, that is correct," Evie replied.

"Annie, why are you home?" Thelma continued.

"Oh, I was working on a story that was only a few blocks away, so I thought I'd stop in for lunch before going back to the office."

Looking across the table, Thelma asked, "How about you, Cecilia?"

Cecilia answered, "I took the day off to get my Missouri driver's license. I've been intending to get one, but just haven't had the time yet."

Gracie, like Deloris, only worked mornings at the switchboard, but she worked on weekends rather than through the week, so she was typically home off and on through the week. She was close to graduating from college with her biology/physiology degree and planned to enter the medical program at General Hospital Training School to be a coroner. Even though General Hospital only offered training for nurses, she felt that the additional knowledge would help her land a coroner's job somewhere.

Deloris started sneezing and discovered that Leota's cat was roaming around their feet. When it tried to jump on the table, which Thelma didn't allow, she shooed it away, saying,

"Leota, you need to leave your cat in your room when you come downstairs or put it outside while we are eating."

Leota mumbled back, "Yes, ma'am." But when she got up, she quickly sat back down, wobbly, with only Deloris noticing.

"So, Evie, tell us what is new with you?" Deloris asked.

"Well, I started taking classes at the Edna Marie Dunn Fashion Design School, and I absolutely love it!" Evie answered.

"What do you love the most about it?" Annie asked, as if in an interview.

"As you know, I enjoy designing my own clothes and Nora's too . But right now, I am learning how to draw the models for the clothes. We start with two triangles, one up and one down, with the points touching. Then we add a circle at the top for the head. From there, we draw the dress design and add the legs if the dress is short."

"Interesting," Cecilia commented. "I wanted to design dresses when I was a little girl."

"You should apply. I can give you the information if you like," Evie offered.

"I would like that," Cecilia said.

"How exciting for you," Gracie commented.

"It is. I just entered a dress design competition where the winner will get an all-expenses-paid trip to Paris and enter a competition over there!"

"That sounds fascinating," Deloris said. "I've always wanted to go to Paris."

When no one was looking, the cat slipped back into the room and stealthily slipped under the table, where it curled up at Leota's feet. Thelma wasn't fond of cats. In the country where she grew up, cats and dogs were outside animals, never inside the house. Of course, Deloris didn't live here then, with her allergies to cats; otherwise, Thelma would never have agreed to it. But Leota pleaded with her when she moved in, and Thelma allowed her to keep the cat in her room. Thelma felt sorry for Leota, whose parents were divorced and whose father was a mean drunk. Leota convinced Thelma that the cat was very docile and would mostly sleep in her room, but recently it would dart out of the room. It had also become mean and attacked people unprovoked, biting and scratching. It even attacked one of Thelma's boarders last year. She told Leota either to control her cat or to get rid of it. Since then, the cat had scratched up the back of Thelma's chair like a scratching post, clawed at and snagged her favorite tablecloth when she had it on the table for a special occasion, and even put a run in Thelma's hosiery.

The final straw for Thelma was when the cat left Leota's feet and jumped up, scratching and biting one of the little girl's legs, making her cry. Often, the girls' legs were scratched up from playing with the cat, but those weren't deep scratches. This attack was vicious and unwarranted, drawing blood. Thelma would not allow the cat to hurt her daughters, so she jumped up and grabbed the broom and shooed it off.

"Leota, get your cat out of here!" she yelled as she ran back to comfort her daughter.

Deloris had been sneezing off and on throughout the lunch, which she always did when the cat was close to her. Leota jumped up and grabbed the cat a little roughly. She took it up to her room and then slammed the door. She returned to the table, but looked a little peaked, and Deloris asked, "Are you feeling okay?"

"I'm just peachy keen," she answered sarcastically.

Thelma told Deloris that Leota had been sick in bed all weekend with a bout of the flu or something. "Are you sure you don't want me to call Dr. Browne, dear? You've been sick since Saturday."

"No!" she quickly answered and shook her head.

Deloris leaned a little closer to Annie to avoid getting too close to Leota in case she was contagious. When everyone dished up their plates, Leota started looking worse and excused herself. She ran back upstairs and slammed her door again.

"I need to tell Leota to go easy on my door," Thelma remarked.

"I'm sorry Leota is sick," Deloris commented. "I noticed she was a little wobbly earlier when she stood up, but I must admit that I am kind of glad she left. I don't want to catch whatever she has. I don't have time to get sick."

Everyone at the table agreed. Then Gracie asked Deloris, "How did your trip up to Jameson go?"

"Yes, how was everyone up home?" Thelma added.

"They're all fine," Deloris replied.

"Did you find anything out about the letter?" Thelma urged.

Deloris told them about the clues she found behind the fire escape, at Grand River, and at the safe deposit box.

"What do you have planned next?" Annie asked.

"I don't know yet. I think I will go see Austin and find out what he thinks about everything. However, I don't want to tell him about the pocket watch I found yet."

"Pocket watch?" Thelma raised an eyebrow in curiosity.

"Oh yes, I found several pieces of jewelry, including a ring that I believe he planned to use in a proposal to Lucy and a pocket watch. I plan to give it to Roy, but I want to ask Mrs. Kerns first."

"I'm sure he would like that," Thelma agreed.

Deloris entertained everyone at the table with tales of her search and with what else she found and where they were hidden.

"It's like a scavenger hunt," Evie voiced.

"It truly is," Deloris agreed. She told them about the key and about opening the safe-deposit box.

"Ooh, what was in there?" Gracie was intrigued.

"There were some interesting papers, but I'm not sure what they mean, so I'm going to take them to the police tomorrow," Deloris answered.

"What kind of papers?" Annie was captivated.

"The normal things you'd find in a safe deposit box, I guess. Stocks, bonds, wills, house key, and birth certificates," Deloris replied.

Evie interrupted, "Reading the papers of a dead man is a little ghoulish!"

"Perhaps," Annie replied, "but finding out what had happened with Dr. Kerns is important enough to go searching for an answer."

"Now you sound just like my mama, Evie," Deloris said with a sly smile, and Thelma groaned.

The telephone rang, and it was Mark Corbane at The Ship. One server had fainted at work, and they wanted to know if Deloris could come in to cover her shift. Deloris agreed, and once she'd hung up, she started gulping down the rest of her meal.

"Aw, I wanted to hear more!" Annie protested. "Promise me, Deloris, that you'll tell me more tomorrow when you get home?"

Deloris promised and then ran upstairs to change. So much for spending the afternoon figuring out what the papers meant! She quickly changed into a spare uniform she kept at home and then was out the door in less than ten minutes.

Annie and Gracie told Thelma, "Go take your nap. We'll clean the kitchen."

It was hard for Thelma to relinquish control over the clean-up because she liked to have things done a certain way, but she was so tired that she accepted their offer.

Chapter Nine
Bob Scott

That late that afternoon when Deloris arrived at The Ship, she jumped right in, helping to serve the customers dinner and after-work cocktails. Things finally slowed down after the dinner crowd, as there weren't that many people who wanted to stay out late on a Tuesday evening, especially with the threat of ice and snow. Just as Deloris thought she'd have some time to think about why David might have wanted her to have those things from the safe deposit box, a familiar face came into The Ship and sat at the bar.

Bob Scott—that was the name. Deloris never forgot a face or a name. Bob Scott was Lucy McCoy's current boyfriend. Deloris had seen him with Lucy at Johnnie Walker's one night a month ago, and then again just last week at another bar. Deloris remembered him from the two times she was with David and he pointed him out to her, along with Lucy. He was about five feet nine inches tall with a muscular, stocky build. He wore his dark brown hair very short, reminiscent of his former military background, she assumed. David told her he was a steelworker at Sheffield Steel when he pointed him out.

It was good that she and David avoided meeting them, because now he didn't know who she was.

She decided not to show that she knew him and to stay incognito, so she just asked, "What'll it be, Joe?"

"Whiskey, straight up, in a dirty glass," he told her.

"That's one order I've never heard," she said. "In a dirty glass?"

"Yeah, it's been that kind of day," he replied.

Deloris served him and went over to clean the booth near the window. Twenty minutes later, Bob ordered another whiskey and then another. After the whiskeys, he started ordering one beer after another.

"Remember, whiskey on beer, rather queer. Beer before whiskey, rather risky?" She said with a wink.

"Yeah, I don't really care anymore," he said, looking down at the bar and shaking his head. Bob looked like a worried man. Deloris wondered why.

Three whiskeys and four beers later, Deloris said, "You look like you've been wrung through the wringer. You okay, mister?"

"You know I didn't kill the guy. I hated him. Oh, I hated him enough to kill him, all right. All Lucy talked about was 'David did this' and 'David did that,' like he was a damn saint. He could do no wrong," Bob sighed. "How does a guy compete with Mr. Perfect Everything?"

Deloris didn't know whether to answer him or just let it go and act indifferent. But she really wanted to hear more about this David. Was he talking about her, David? After waiting a few moments, it appeared Bob didn't want to talk anymore, so she nudged him on. "Oh?" she said in a questioning tone. Deloris decided now was the perfect time to wash the glasses in the bar sink, as it would give her a reason to stand in front of him, hoping he would say more.

He thought for a minute and then said, "Nothing. Never mind."

Deloris had been a barmaid for a few years now, and she'd learned long ago never to push for answers. The customers didn't like that; they'd only talk when they were ready. Usually, though, the reason they came to the bar to drink alone was because they wanted a sympathetic ear. She'd let Bob spill to her when he was ready.

Deloris went about tending to other customers and tried to look unconcerned. When she returned, he ordered another beer and mumbled, "I only wanted to scare him."

Wait, what did he say? Deloris's mind started spinning. Was he still talking about David? It was her David; she was pretty sure. He wanted to scare him? How did he scare him? Did he kill David? Accidentally? On purpose? She had so many questions.

"Scare who, darlin'?" Deloris said, acting as calm and nonchalant as she could muster, and then served him another beer. She stood there, waiting for his reply, and finally, it came.

Looking into his beer, Bob said softly, "I went to his house and told him I didn't want to see him anywhere around Lucy. I told him, 'Don't look at her, don't talk to her, don't even think about her. Back off or I'll put a slug in you.' He slammed the door in my face, and I lost it. I started punching the door with my fist, screaming and yelling at the top of my lungs."

"Who are we talking about, sweetie?" Deloris interrupted.

He continued as if he hadn't heard her, dropping his head onto his arm on the bar. "And then I found out afterward she went to see him when I told her not to."

"Went to see who?" Deloris asked.

Bob lifted his head and screamed, "David! David Kerns! The

damn near perfect man!" as he fell off the bar stool.

There it was! She had his story with only a little coaxing. Now, she didn't believe he killed David because she didn't think he would have had the patience to wait for poison. He would have shot him, fast and easy, but it sounded like Lucy had been hanging around David even after they broke up and comparing Bob to him. There might be something there to look into.

Deloris ran around the bar to help him get up and asked Willie to help her. She turned to RayAnn and said, "Will you call a taxi and cover for me!"

"Let's get you home," she said to Bob as she took off her apron and grabbed her coat and purse. Then she gathered his change on the bar before she and Willie walked him outside.

On the sidewalk, Willie held one arm, and Deloris held the other. Bob continued mumbling, "But I didn't kill him. Honest, I didn't." He said, looking from Willie to Deloris with his bleary eyes. Then he stumbled, and they caught him before he fell.

"Yes, yes, I know. I believe you," Deloris said as the taxi arrived, and she got him inside with Willie's help, then hopped in beside him. "What's your address?"

"1716 Bellefontaine Avenue," came the slurred reply as he fell asleep on her shoulder.

Her mind was going in several directions as she replayed his conversation. She needed to tell Austin about this and find a way to talk with Lucy. Maybe she'd be at this address.

When the taxi pulled up, she paid for the ride with the money she had gathered from Bob's bar change. She then asked the driver to help her get Bob up the stairs to his front door and then wait for her to return to take her back to the bar. It was pretty late now, and she didn't want to have to make her way back on foot.

Lucy flung the door open as they approached and started screaming at Bob, "Where in the hell did you go?" Lucy ignored the taxi driver, but as soon as she saw Deloris, her eyes narrowed and a wave of jealousy loomed across her face. "Who are you?" she sneered. "And what have you done to Bob?"

Apparently, Lucy was so mad that she didn't recognize Deloris from when David had introduced them a year ago. She was a curvaceous redhead with a knockout figure and still had too much makeup even though she was at home.

"Bob was at The Ship, where I work, and when he fell off the barstool, I got him a taxi and brought him home," Deloris replied.

Lucy appeared not to believe her at first. Then she replied, "The crumb didn't tell me where he was going. We had an argument, and he just stormed out the door."

The three of them managed to get Bob to a bed, and the taxi driver returned to his cab.

"I'll be down in a minute," Deloris told the driver, and gave him a coin so that he'd wait. Deloris hoped that if she stayed for a minute longer, Lucy would say something else. She offered a touch of camaraderie by saying, "When my boyfriend and I get into a fight, it can sometimes be a doozy, and I don't see him for a day or two. I just leave him alone to cool off, and he eventually comes back."

Lucy softened and said, "Yeah, he has a terrible temper,

but other than that, he's a good guy. I've dated better and I've dated worse."

Deloris smiled, "Me, too."

Lucy sighed, "It's just that I often need to apologize for his behavior. Like last week."

"Last week?" Deloris asked.

"Oh, it was nothing. Bob threatened my ex-boyfriend, and then I had to find my ex to apologize for Bob," Lucy shrugged. "It was embarrassing, you know."

"I understand." Deloris said, "I've had to apologize for my boyfriends, too." Lucy's clock chimed midnight, reminding Deloris that she had a taxi waiting. "I've got to get back to work and back to the taxi before I acquire the national debt."

"Hold on a minute," Lucy said as she grabbed her purse and dug into it for her coin purse. She offered Deloris some money to help with the taxi.

Deloris thanked her and headed down the front porch steps. Then she stopped and turned back toward Lucy.

"Oh, I almost forgot. Here is the change that Bob left on the bar. I used some of it to pay for the taxi here." Deloris held out her hand with the money.

"You can keep the change, and the money I gave you. You earned it," Lucy said with a small smile.

On the ride back to The Ship, Deloris contemplated what she had learned. Apparently, Bob saw—or at least suspected—that Lucy was still with David and then threatened David. Then Lucy went to David to apologize. Interesting. She wondered when that had happened, if that was on February

13th. Austin said that another hotel guest overheard a lover's spat outside David's room the night he was murdered. But Deloris thought, how could Lucy have known that David was at the hotel?

And while Deloris didn't think that Bob had killed David, she had to at least consider it as a possibility. Why was Bob so suspicious of Lucy and David in the first place? David obviously loved Lucy at one time, and the engagement ring he'd bought showed he intended to marry her. Maybe the engagement ring was the clue David left for Deloris in the safe deposit box. But if it was a clue, what did it mean?

When Deloris got back to The Ship, there was only half an hour till closing, and it was pretty empty. Deloris leaned on the bar and found a piece of scratch paper to write another plan.

- Note to self: Keep a scratchpad handy at all times.
- Give Austin and Big Jim the information I learned about Lucy and Bob, and tell them about the contents of the safe deposit box.
- Go to David's house and tell Austin.
- Interview David's neighbors to see if any of them saw Bob or Lucy at the house and when?

Deloris crossed out "tell Austin" as she figured Austin would arrest her before he'd let her break in. Maybe Annie would go with her?

Chapter Ten
Dr. Cramer

Early the next morning, after breakfast, Deloris ran upstairs to get ready for work at the switchboard and found Leota was in the bathroom, so she had to wait. Leota stayed home with the flu again that day. Oh, how Deloris wished she could stay home and sleep, but she had too much to do. Before she left for work, she told Thelma that Leota was sick again, so Dr. Browne was finally called. Dr. Browne made an early-morning house call to tend to Leota, and Deloris ran into him on the stairs when she was leaving for work. The look on his face made her skin crawl, as she remembered the check-up he gave her when she got her server's permit. She didn't envy Leota for this doctor's visit.

On Deloris's break at the switchboard, she called the Pickwick Hotel, where one of her boyfriends, George Packard, was a bellhop. She was still annoyed that George hadn't asked her out for Valentine's Day, but it was just as well, since she didn't feel like celebrating after David's death. The operator connected her to the front desk of the Pickwick, and the concierge answered. Luckily, George had just finished taking a guest's luggage out to a taxi, and the concierge flagged him down and put him on the line.

"Hello, Georgie. Do you have a minute to talk?" Deloris asked.

"For you, sweetheart, I have all the time in the world," George replied smoothly.

"Oh, you have time now," Deloris pouted, "but you didn't on Valentine's Day?"

"I told you, if you volunteer to work as a busboy when the restaurant is busy, you make dough. And that's more dough to spend on you later, dollface."

"Save it, lover boy," Deloris replied. "You didn't even call me all day."

"I left you a card and a box of chocolates," he pleaded. "Okay, what can I do to make it up to you?" George cooed. "How about a big night out? I'll take you out to eat and then to the bar at Union Station. You can order as many Tom Collins or Rum and Cokes as you want. We'll do it up right, kid."

"Well..." Deloris said coquettishly. Even though it was over the telephone line, Deloris batted her eyes anyway, hoping it would come through in her voice. "Maybe you could make it up to me in another way. Can you look up someone at the hotel for me? And we could do a night out on the town in a week or two, when I can get someone to cover for me at The Ship."

"Easy as pie," George said. "What do you want to know?"

Deloris relaxed a little. She knew George wasn't supposed to give out information about the hotel guests, but evidently, he was willing to bend the rules to please her. Deloris crossed her fingers for luck. "Could you see if Dr. Myron Cramer is still at the hotel?"

"Another man, dollface?" Now George was definitely curious. "Say, why'd you want to know about a doctor?"

Deloris sighed impatiently. "It's nothing like that, Georgie. It's because he might know a friend of mine. The one who died in your hotel, Dr. Kerns."

"Do you think he might have the lowdown on his death?" George asked.

"I don't know, but I want to talk to him to see if he knows anything. I don't know how long he's staying in Kansas City."

George checked the hotel register. "Dr. Cramer is still checked in, but his reservation is only through tomorrow."

"Swell!" Deloris said. "Can you have the waiters keep an eye out for him until I can get there? I'm hoping to catch him while he's eating lunch."

"If you'll forgive me for Valentine's Day, I will," George countered.

Deloris laughed. "All is forgiven, as long as we still have a night out."

"It's a date," George said. "And I'll make sure I find the doctor and point him out to you myself when you get here."

"You're a peach," Deloris replied. "I'll be there in a jiffy."

When her shift was over at the switchboard, Deloris took the streetcar to the Pickwick Hotel, which encompassed an entire city block, stretching from 9th to 10th Streets on McGee with the Greyhound bus terminal, several retail businesses, offices, the KMBZ radio station, a cafeteria, a garage and, of course, the hotel. She'd been there before to see George, but every time she walked in, she had to admire how elegant and massive it was with its colossal marble columns leading up to the white ceilings, inset with eight ornate panels. She always had to remember to be careful not to slip on the highly polished floors. Today, though, it just made her sad to enter the place where David breathed his last breath. This was where someone had poisoned him.

As Deloris approached the hotel, she saw her boyfriend taking a guest's luggage outside to the curb to a waiting taxicab. George took his tip from the customer, closed the taxi door, and then turned to see Deloris walking up. He gave her a big hug.

"How are you doing, dollface?" he asked as he draped an arm around her shoulders.

"I'm fine, Georgie, but have you seen Dr. Cramer?" She replied.

"Yeah, he just came down to the restaurant for lunch. You've got plenty of time to catch him."

George started flirting and was more interested in making time with Deloris than pointing out the doctor, but Deloris dragged him inside and told him, "Shake a leg! I don't have a lot of time before he may leave. Point him out to me, please."

"Gee, Deloris, you're more interested in the doctor than me." George pretended to be upset and gave her a puppy-dog look. "I'm heartbroken."

Deloris gave him a look of annoyance back. "I think you'll survive. Now, point him out to me, and I'll give you plenty of time on our date, alright?"

He sighed sadly, shaking his head. "You're a cruel dame, Deloris."

At the entrance to the restaurant, George caught the eye of one of the waiters, who came over and discreetly pointed out where the doctor had been seated for lunch. Shooing George back to the concierge desk and his job, Deloris walked over to the man. He was in his late fifties or early sixties, with glasses he wore halfway down his nose, exposing his dark brown, weary eyes. He was bald, but his gray eyebrows and mustache defied his youthful face. He was short, with a slight paunch and an apparent penchant for wearing Hawaiian shirts.

Dr. Cramer raised his eyes and saw a beautiful woman approaching. He rose courteously as Deloris neared his table.

"To what do I owe the pleasure of your company?" he said respectfully.

"Dr. Cramer," Deloris said, "I'm a friend of Dr. David Kerns. I was hoping to talk to you for a minute."

"Certainly," said Dr. Cramer. "Might I have your name?"

"Miss Deloris Markham."

"How do you do, Miss Markham?" Dr. Cramer replied. "Please have a seat. Have you had lunch?"

"No, but that's alright. I'm sorry to bother you at lunch," Deloris said. She took a notepad and a pen out of her purse. "Do you mind if I ask you some questions?"

"Please be my guest and have lunch with me. We can talk while eating. I'd appreciate the company of such a beautiful young lady."

"Thank you; that would be really nice," Deloris replied, blushing.

A waiter came by, poured them both a glass of water, and took their orders. When the waiter left, the doctor turned to Deloris, saying, "First, I want to express my sympathies. David was a talented researcher, and the world is much poorer for his loss."

Deloris nodded, a little misty-eyed. "I've known him all my

life. He was like another big brother to me."

"I am so sorry, my dear. I'm still shaken up myself." Dr. Cramer replied. "Now, how may I be of assistance to you?"

"Could you tell me about David's last night?" Deloris asked.

"Certainly, but first let me say that I do not know why David would commit suicide. When we talked the night before, he seemed in good spirits and excited about working on the research project for the James and James Institute."

"What did you talk about?" Deloris asked.

"Well, we'd spent most of the evening making a plan for the research into Blue Mass, but then David started feeling ill and went to his room," Dr. Cramer said.

"So, you didn't talk about anything else but the research?" Deloris asked.

"No," Dr. Cramer continued once the waiter had left. "I had hoped we were going to figure out how and when David would move to New York City when we talked the next morning."

Deloris wasn't sure how much of a clue the research or the trip to New York City would be, but Dr. Cramer didn't seem to think anything out of the ordinary had been discussed. "Time to try a different tactic," Deloris thought.

The waiter arrived, bringing Virginia ham, sweet potatoes, green beans, and piping hot rolls straight out of the oven. It looked delicious, but Deloris was too focused on the conversation to eat much.

"Dr. Cramer," Deloris asked, "how did you meet David in the first place?" Even though she had heard David's version, she thought it wouldn't hurt to hear Dr. Cramer's version. Maybe he'd remember something, or... Deloris was getting stumped. Maybe this was a dead end.

"I'd already started the research project on the effectiveness of Blue Mass, with its potential complications and side effects, but I had let go one doctor working on the project," Dr. Cramer explained. "He seemed to be a talented researcher at first, but it turned out he'd taken credit for another's research. When I found that out, I fired him. Once he was gone, we needed to hire a new researcher, and Dr. Kerns was the best candidate."

This was interesting. This person may have had a reason to want David out of the way, so that he could get his job back, maybe? Though she didn't see how this person would even have known to be mad at David if he'd been fired before David had been hired, unless he met David or heard about him from someone still working on the project?

"How did you find David?" Deloris asked.

"Did you know David published an article on Blue Mass in one of the most prestigious American medical journals?" Dr. Cramer asked.

"Yes, he told me about that months ago, when he sent it off," Deloris replied.

"It was a brilliant article; I had the entire research team read it when it came out," Dr. Cramer said. "After that, I discovered the problems with Johnson and fired him. I mean this person. I didn't plan to reveal his name."

"That's okay. I understand. I think David may have mentioned him." Deloris said encouragingly.

Dr. Cramer continued, "I decided to see if David would be willing to move to New York to join our project." He paused for a minute. "Now ... I'll have to find someone else."

"I hope you find someone good," Deloris said, while her mind raced. So, this Dr. Johnson would have known about David coming. She made a note to ask Austin to check his background.

She hesitated for a minute, but then told the doctor to see his reaction. "You should know I don't believe David committed suicide. And I intend to find out who killed him."

Dr. Cramer appeared shaken and taken aback by her statement. Then he said, "Why do you say that? I suspected it wasn't suicide, but to hear you say it confirms my fears."

He didn't look like he was faking it, but even Dr. Cramer could be the killer. He didn't have a motive, but you never know. "Everyone is a suspect at this point, so his name goes on the list," she thought.

"I had lunch with David often, including the Thursday before he met with you, and I saw his excitement in starting the research with James and James. That's the main reason I don't believe he committed suicide," she explained. "Also, I heard the initial coroner's report. They think he might have been poisoned."

Startled, Dr. Cramer asked, "But who would want to kill David?"

"That's what I'm trying to find out," she replied. Dr. Cramer looked thoughtful. Then Deloris saw a look of realization cross his face as he raised one eyebrow and cocked his head slightly. "What's on your mind?" she asked quickly.

"Oh, nothing," he replied.

"Please, if you know anything," Deloris said. "I need your

help to find David's killer."

"I don't want to cast aspersions," Dr. Cramer replied, "or make false accusations in case it is nothing. Besides, the person I'm thinking about was in New York City and not here. He couldn't have murdered David."

"But isn't it better," Deloris offered, "to look into everyone and find them innocent than to miss finding the guilty party because you don't want to accuse them? Is it this Dr. Johnson?"

With resignation in his voice, Dr. Cramer proceeded to tell her more about Dr. Johnson. "When I fired Donald Johnson, he started sending me threatening notes, telling me I would regret firing him. That he would expose me as a fraud and that my research was a joke. He even accused me of having false credentials. Of course, none of that was true. It was merely a scare tactic that Johnson used. And I wasn't the only one to get notes. Everyone on the Blue Mass research team got notes," Dr. Cramer sighed. "Somehow Johnson found out that we were going to hire Kerns, and he mentioned Kerns in one note he sent me."

"What did he say about David?" She wrote this down in her notepad, too.

"Oh, he said his article about Blue Mass was plagiarized." Dr. Cramer looked down and shook his head sadly when he said this.

"Did you tell the police?" Deloris asked. She put the notepad down and took a bite of the ham.

"No," Dr. Cramer replied. "I thought if I just ignored him, he would eventually stop."

"He certainly sounds like a mean, despicable man," Deloris

said. “Maybe one who would stop at nothing to get his way, maybe even kill?”

“Perhaps. I hope not,” Dr. Cramer said. “I would hate if my hiring David caused him to be murdered, if he was murdered.”

Deloris looked at Dr. Cramer and then offered, “Will you still be around today? I plan to tell the police what we discussed and would like for them to talk with you as well.”

Dr. Cramer replied, “Oh yes, the police telephoned me yesterday and have already asked that I remain in town for a few days so that they can talk with me. I was already planning on staying at least until after the funeral. This reminds me I need to extend my room reservation.”

As Deloris took another bite of ham, she wondered if there was anything else she should ask the doctor, but she couldn’t come up with anything. Disappointed that there didn’t seem to be any additional clues to be found, Deloris finished eating her food and thanked Dr. Cramer for inviting her to lunch.

When Dr. Cramer held her chair for her to stand up, he flinched and his jaw dropped open as a look of shock crossed his face, and Deloris followed his gaze. Across the room, a tall, thin man wearing a gray suit was making his way toward Dr. Cramer. He had a military gait and stared straight ahead through wire-rimmed glasses. The look on his face was pure loathing.

As he approached, Dr. Cramer said angrily, “What are you doing here?”

With a smirk, the man exaggeratedly tipped his hat to Deloris and then replied, “I saw the news. Looks like you’re short a doc, doc.”

Dr. Cramer turned towards Deloris and gave her a pointed look. "Miss Markham, thank you for joining me for lunch. I think you need to be on your way now. Dr. Johnson and I have things to discuss."

"Dr. Johnson! So he is in town," she thought to herself. Dr. Johnson had dark brown hair had hints of graying temples, and his steel-blue eyes narrowed to slits as he glanced at her with an air of annoyance.

Deloris said, "Goodbye, and thank you again for lunch." Then she pretended to walk away. She stopped after a few steps, hiding behind the nearest column, and faked needing to straighten the back line in her stocking, trying to hear any conversation between the two men.

"Again, what are you doing here?" Cramer hissed.

"I'm a guest of the hotel, and it's a free country, isn't it?" Johnson replied.

Dr. Cramer, looking both annoyed and a bit frightened, stormed out of the dining room, leaving Johnson standing there staring after him with the same smirk on his face.

Deloris slipped out of the dining room when Dr. Cramer left. She vowed to report everything she found out about Dr. Donald Johnson and ask Austin to look into him as the number one suspect. She had a suspect now, one that had a reason to want David gone if for no other reason than to hamper Dr. Cramer's research, and who was mysteriously in Kansas City at the right time.

Before leaving the hotel, she stopped at the front desk. The front desk clerk asked George to watch the desk, and he complied. When she left, George tried to flirt again, but Deloris had no time to spare. He leaned in for a kiss.

"Georgie, I will not kiss you in public, and especially not while you're working. Besides, I have to get to the police station—I found something out!"

"What?" George asked.

"I can't tell you everything right now, but I need you to do me a favor."

"Anything for you, Deloris."

"There's someone here at the hotel that's supposed to be in New York City, and he was mad at David," she explained.

"Gosh, you found the murderer!" George was impressed.

"Maybe, but I've got to tell the police and have him investigated," Deloris said. "Could you find out what room a Dr. Donald Johnson is in and then keep an eye on him for me? Tell me every one of his movements?"

"Absolutely!" George's eyes sparkled. "I'll get all the staff to look out for him, too." With a gleam in his eye, he said, "Let's see." He took a peek into the ledger. "Here he is!" he proudly exclaimed. "He is in Room 204."

"Perfect!" Deloris said. "Now I've got to dash. Thank you and goodbye!" She gave him a quick peck on the cheek, and he put his hand on the spot as if to hold it there and grinned.

Deloris exited the Pickwick Hotel and thanked her lucky stars for the perfect timing, as the streetcar was coming down the street, headed for her stop. She could have walked the few blocks to the police station, but the streetcar was faster. She jumped on board and headed for the station to tell Austin and Big Jim what she had learned.

Chapter Eleven
The Police Station

Deloris walked into the police station and sighed. Joey Crabtree was working at the front desk again. She didn't have any baked goods with her to bribe him, but this time, she had important facts and evidence to share. He'd have to let her through to talk to Austin and Big Jim.

"Joey," she said, "I need to speak to Austin or Big Jim."

"Did you bring any more cinnamon rolls?" Joey asked hopefully.

"Am I carrying a bakery box?" Deloris looked at him, exasperated. "You'll never make detective if you don't use your eyes."

"I—no, it just, um." Joey was flustered.

"I've just found something out that they need to hear," she said.

"I'm sorry, Deloris, but you can't see them right now."

Deloris gave Joey her sternest look. "It's important. It's about Dr. Kerns. You need to let me go back there."

"No, no, it's not that," Joey replied. "They're in a meeting with the chief right now."

"Do you know when they'll get out?"

"No, but if you wait here, I'll let you know as soon as they get done," Joey promised.

Deloris sat down on the wooden visitors' bench. She crossed her legs, which made her skirt slide up a little, showing off her calves. Joey gulped and then stared back down at the ledger on his desk. She looked around the room, but the station was quiet. Nothing to watch and no one to talk to. Impatiently, she started tapping her painted red fingernails on the arm of the bench. Joey was avoiding her eyes, studiously writing in the ledger. Deloris dug into her purse and took out her makeup. She opened her compact and started powdering her nose. Joey looked up. When she was satisfied with her powder, she took out her lipstick. Propping the compact mirror on the bench arm where she could see herself, she slid a small brush out of its case. With the lipstick in one hand and the brush in the other, she re-outlined her lips. Joey was frozen, staring. Deloris mashed her lips together, making the mmm sound as she did it, too, and then made a move with her lips to check her pout. Perfect. She closed the compact with a loud click, which startled Joey, who turned red and mumbled an excuse. He then hurried into another room of the police station, out of sight.

Deloris smiled and put the compact, lipstick, and brush away. "Mission accomplished," she murmured as she got up and strolled back to the room where the detectives' desks were. She'd settled into Austin's chair and was reviewing her notes when Austin and Big Jim came in.

"How'd you get back here?" Austin asked. "Wasn't there someone at the front desk?"

Deloris simply said, "Joey." And then she smiled.

It took a second, but both Austin and Big Jim figured it out, nodded to each other, and gave a chuckle.

"You," Big Jim said, "are a pip. You really know how to get

your way."

Austin grinned. "You know, when we were in training, no one ever taught us about how to deal with dames like you."

Deloris smiled back. "Anyway, boys, I had to talk to you. Have I got news for you!" she exclaimed.

"What's your story, morning glory?" Austin asked.

"Well, to start off, I had a humdinger of a conversation last night at work," Deloris replied. She told them both about what happened at The Ship. "So, Bob Scott, this steelworker, was full of hooch and complaining about how his dame went to see David a few nights ago?"

"There are lots of Davids in Kansas City, Deloris," Big Jim said with a wink at Austin.

"Yes, but I'd seen him with Lucy before—I remembered his face. I saw the two of them when David and I went out for dinner a time or two, but David attempted to avoid them, so I don't think they saw me," Deloris said. "When I took Bob home in a taxi last night..." Austin cut her off from finishing what she was about to say.

"You got into a taxi with a drunk, possibly dangerous stranger last night? Deloris!" Austin said with consternation. She could tell that he was not pleased with the revelation.

"Relax, copper, I can handle a sozzled man." Deloris winked and slightly shook her head in annoyance. "Anyway, I dropped him off at his place, and Lucy was there. It was Lucy McCoy, the same Lucy that David was dating. Luckily, she didn't recognize me from the one time we met."

"So, Lucy was making time with two men?" Big Jim asked.

"No, at least I don't think so. David and Lucy broke up several months ago. But Lucy, well, she's the kind of a kitten that'll drink milk from any saucer that's offered. I don't know when she got her claws into Bob Scott."

"Lucy McCoy?" Austin paused. "That name sounds familiar." Austin turned to Big Jim and said, "Let's grab Joey and have him go through the books for Lucy McCoy's name. Maybe she's in there and that's why her name sounds familiar to me."

"Yep," Big Jim replied, and walked to the door to call out, "Officer Crabtree."

There was the sound of hurrying footsteps, and Joey's face appeared at the door. "Yes, sir?" Joey said. Then he saw Deloris, lowered his head as he shook it, expecting to get into trouble for her presence.

"Get your mitts on the beauty contest books. Look for a Lucy McCoy," Big Jim said.

"On it, sir," Joey replied. Then he stopped. "Uh, beauty contest books? Where do I find them?"

"Rap sheets!" Austin and Big Jim said in unison.

"Oh, yes," Joey replied and promptly left.

Austin pulled out his notebook, saying, "I'll go over to Bob Scott's place and get his story. What was that address, Deloris?"

"1716 Bellefontaine Avenue."

"Thanks," Austin said. "I'll ring you later and catch you up."

"Hold on, I've got more to tell you!" Deloris interrupted.

Austin and Big Jim stopped mid-step and turned to face her.

Delighted with their confusion, Deloris announced, "I met with Dr. Cramer today."

"You what?" Austin and Big Jim both exclaimed.

"Deloris, stay out of police business. Leave the investigating to us." He didn't call her DeDe when he was around Big Jim or the other police officers.

"Now, boys, you know I can't do that," Deloris replied with a coquettish grin.

Chief Douglas came out of his office to see why Big Jim and Austin were yelling.

Deloris then started telling them about Dr. Donald Johnson showing up at the hotel and how he had threatened both Dr. Cramer and David. "Dr. Johnson had a reason to kill David. And no reason to be in Kansas City."

The detectives and the chief exchanged glances. Then the chief said, "Well, guys, what do you think?"

"Alright, we'll talk to him, too," Austin said.

"And we are already talking to Dr. Cramer," Big Jim added.

"Keen work, Deloris," Austin said. "Is there anything else you've sneaked around and found out since yesterday?"

"Just one more thing," Deloris added. "Johnson's room at the Pickwick Hotel is #204."

"How? Oh, never mind," Big Jim stopped himself.

A figure walked up behind them and stood near Big Jim.

"Sorry to cut in on your conversation, but I've brought

over an update to the coroner's report." It was the coroner's assistant, Carolyn Bechtel, and with her was another woman. She introduced her to everyone. "I'd like to introduce my new assistant trainee, Gracie Burnett. We found, Gracie and I, that is," nodding to Gracie, "found more information on the Kerns autopsy."

"Hey, we know you," Austin said with surprise.

Then, he and Big Jim offered their congratulations to both women, but Deloris stood there for a moment, stunned. When she looked at the other woman with Carolyn, she couldn't believe her eyes. It was her housemate. Gracie was wearing a lab coat and looked very professional with a big smile. Deloris regained her composure and gave Gracie a small wave. Gracie waved back and nodded.

"Gracie?" Deloris moved to stand next to her. "I did not know you were up for becoming an assistant to the assistant coroner. You kept this a secret from everyone!"

"I just got the job offer this morning. I was afraid to say anything in case I jinxed it and it didn't happen."

"Congratulations. I am so happy for you," Deloris gave her a quick hug. "You are well on your way to realizing your dream of becoming the coroner."

"Thank you," Gracie replied, slightly embarrassed. "But I still have a long way to go."

"I don't know about that," Carolyn broke in. "It's a hard nut to crack, advancing into the upper echelon of the coroner's job. I've been at it for years, but Gracie here is brilliant. If anyone can make it, I'm sure she can."

The Chief broke the mood with this: "Now that all the

introductions and accolades are over, what did you find, Miss Bechtel?"

Deloris mouthed to Gracie, "We'll talk more later."

"Yes, we have a revision to the original coroner's report," Carolyn replied.

"What changed?" Chief Douglas asked.

"The report is still correct. Arsenic poisoning killed David Kerns, but it wasn't taken with his meal, apparently, as Miss Burnett discovered." Carolyn looked at Gracie appreciatively.

Deloris, Austin, Big Jim and the chief looked at each other, a bit dumbfounded by the revelation.

"The arsenic poisoning was found in the coffeepot and coffee cup in his room. But we also found an excessive amount of mercury in his system," Carolyn continued.

"So, he also overdosed on mercury?" Big Jim asked.

"No, the mercury appeared to have been taken over a longer period of time," she replied.

"So, someone was poisoning David slowly with mercury, and then someone else poisoned him quickly with arsenic?" Austin asked.

"The coroner's office can't say if they were two different individuals," Carolyn replied.

"I know that!" Austin replied, slightly agitated. "I was just thinking out loud." Then, realizing he had said it rather gruffly to Carolyn, he softened and apologized.

"Oh, yes." Carolyn looked embarrassed, realizing he wasn't asking her the question, but then she became slightly agitated.

"It's possible."

Austin continued with his theory. "So, it could be someone who tired of the slow approach and then offed him quickly—or—two different people who were poisoners?!" Austin looked floored as he realized he could be looking for more than one person.

"You got it," Carolyn said, and then she and Gracie quickly exited the room.

Deloris was stunned. That anyone would want to murder David was hard enough to believe, but two people wanted him dead? She shook her head in disbelief. The fact that someone had been poisoning him slowly with mercury was beyond anything. It was also very cruel, given his research into Blue Mass and its mercury content.

"Can you beat that?" Big Jim stated.

Austin said. "This case is getting all balled up."

"Sounds like you two have a lot of work ahead of you," Chief Douglas commented.

Big Jim replied, "Let's get the lead out and check this out."

Chapter Twelve
The Pickwick Staff

As Deloris sat in her room that afternoon thinking about David, she remembered she had forgotten to tell Big Jim and Austin about the safe deposit box contents. She would try to remember to tell them when she saw the duo next. Sitting there, another thought popped in Deloris's head: she needed to go back to the Pickwick and replay the events from the night before David was found dead. She needed to see if Georgie could help her talk with other staff who were on duty that night.

When Deloris came downstairs, she saw Leota just getting home from her work as a maid at the President Hotel. It was a little later than usual, but maybe she was making up for the time off she was sick. Deloris thought she would ask her about who on the hotel staff may have interacted with David and maybe saw the murderer.

"Hey Leota, I'm glad to see you are finally feeling better. Can you help me figure something out? Can you give me an idea of the different staff at a hotel who may interact with the guests in their rooms or near the rooms?"

Leota looked at her for a moment as if she hadn't heard her and then hesitantly asked, "Why do you want to know that?"

"I need to establish a timeline for David's — I mean, Dr. Kerns — last night alive, and I hope to ask the staff for help."

"Oh, okay," Leota replied as she took off her coat and became lost in thought for a moment. "Well, let's see, the clerk at the front desk and the bellhop. Then there is the elevator operator."

Deloris added, "What about a maid? Would he possibly have interacted with a maid?"

"Oh yes, silly me. I completely forgot that a maid may have brought him towels or something," Leota answered as she watched Deloris turn and hurriedly yell thanks and dash off to catch a bus to the hotel.

At the Pickwick, Deloris walked in and saw George talking to the desk clerk, a pretty young woman of about twenty. A flash of jealousy crossed her mind, but she didn't have time to worry about that right now. She needed George's help. Besides, she had more than one boyfriend, so he could have more than one girlfriend, she surmised. When she left Jameson, she had one boy's senior ring, another boy's senior pin, and another proposing marriage to her. Her solution to the dilemma was to leave them all in the country and head for the big city.

When George saw Deloris, he jolted upright and straightened his cap with a gulp. He walked toward her and started giving her his excuse. "Deloris, I...I. Look, I'm not dizzy for that dame."

Deloris brushed it off and said, "Don't blow your wig. That isn't important right now. I need your help."

Surprised, yet relieved he was off the hook, George said, "Yeah sure, anything you need, doll."

"First," Deloris instructed, counting on her fingers, "I need you to keep an eye on Johnson and tell me when he leaves the hotel and if he checks out. Second, I need to talk with anyone on the staff who may have seen or talked with David Kerns the night before he was found dead."

"You got it, doll. Let me find out who worked that night. I'll be right back."

Five minutes later, George returned with a list and handed it to Deloris. He told her she was in luck because most of them were working this evening too. She asked him to go with her to help find and talk with each of them.

"Sure thing, kitten. I get off in twenty minutes and I'll take you around."

Deloris looked around the lobby and decided to talk to the desk clerk while George wrapped up his duties.

Flinching slightly, the pretty, young desk clerk watched Deloris walk toward her.

"Look, honey, I know he is a crumb and flirts with all the girls. I must be off my nut to date him. I don't hold it against you. I need to ask you a couple of questions," Deloris stated as she placed two bits on the counter. That was all she had in her purse.

"Oh, uh, okay," the girl responded, looking around and then sliding the coin towards herself.

Looking at the list George just gave her, Deloris said, "Are you Ann Green and were you working here on February 13th?"

"Yes," the desk clerk hesitantly replied.

"Do you remember when Dr. David Kerns checked in and what room he was in?"

"Yes, he was in room 222."

Deloris was surprised that she had given her this information willingly, and that she knew the room number so quickly. "She must be afraid of me," Deloris thought with a smile.

"Can you tell me if anyone was with him?" Deloris continued.

"Are you the police?" Ann's eyes narrowed.

"No, but I work at the police station with the police as a consultant." Deloris again left out the part that she worked at the switchboard.

"Oh, okay. He checked in alone, but I saw a dame trying to talk with him outside our front doors there." She nodded in the direction of the doors and continued, "She followed him in, but he kept walking away from her."

Excited at this revelation, Deloris continued. "What did she look like? Do you remember?"

"She was wearing her glad rags - a flowing green gown with matching shoes. I noticed because she looked all dressed up, and we didn't have an event here that night. It was the following night."

Deloris wrote that down, but then said, "Great, but do you remember what she looked like?"

"Oh, let's see. She had fire-red hair, a good figure and orange-red lipstick with fingernails to match."

"Thanks!" Deloris responded. She figured that Lucy must have followed him to the hotel.

Ann continued, "I saw her later, too, but she had changed her fancy clothes and wore a simple dress."

Surprised, Deloris said, "About what time was that?"

“About 9 or 9:30, I think,” Ann replied.

“Excellent.” Deloris scribbled this additional fact on her notepad. “Do you remember anyone else talking to him?”

That sounded like Dr. Cramer. “Thank you. You’ve been a great help.”

“Thank you. You’ve been a great help.” She must be referring to Dr. Cramer, Deloris noted.

George entered the foyer and walked towards Deloris. He tried to put his arm around her, but she shrugged it off. Then he stood there looking down, until she said, “Come on, let’s get crackin’.”

The first person they talked to was the elevator operator. He remembered Dr. Kerns because he slipped him a sawbuck to tell him when Dr. Cramer arrived. Then he said that another man, tall, military type, jumped in the elevator when he was taking Kerns up to his floor. They had an angry exchange of words that continued when they got off the elevator.

“Do you remember what was said?” Deloris asked excitedly. This is proof that Dr. Johnson could have murdered David.

“Something about stealing a job. I didn’t really listen too closely. I was just ready to get them off of my elevator before a fight broke out.”

“What time was this?”

“Shortly after nine o’clock.”

“Okay, thank you. You’ve been a big help,” Deloris said.

Next, they went looking for the maid, Aline, or Alley Cat, as George called her, but her shift was over at the same time as George’s, and she had left for home already. George thought she lived on Strawberry Hill in Kansas City, Kansas, but he didn't know the exact address.

"Well, that was a bust until we can talk with her."

They moved on to talk to the waiter in the restaurant.

"Deloris, this is Raphael," George said as he introduced the waiter.

"Nice to meet you, Raphael," Deloris said as she offered her hand to shake his.

He whispered back, "Really, my name is Ralph, but the patrons here prefer the exotic, so I changed it." He smiled as he took her hand and turned it to kiss the top.

"Hey, that's my gal," George protested.

"Sorry. Mea culpa," Ralph said as he backed away from Deloris with a sly smile. "What can I do for you?"

"I have some questions I'd like to ask you," Deloris answered.

"I don't want the Matre d' to see me not working. How about I seat you somewhere we can talk quietly?" Ralph offered.

He sat them at a table in the back, where he offered Deloris something to eat. She declined, but agreed to a cup of coffee.

Deloris asked him, "Do you remember Dr. Kerns and Dr. Cramer eating in the restaurant on Thursday, February 13th?"

"I do, because they were two people sitting at a table for four, but they had papers and files covering the table, and some papers had to be moved when the food arrived," Ralph answered.

"What time was that?" Deloris asked.

"About seven o'clock," Ralph replied.

He told Deloris, "They sat at the table until about nine o'clock when the younger gentleman left, saying he was sick. He looked sick, too. The police talked with me and the kitchen staff two days later, and they checked out our garbage. But of course, all the food waste from that night was dumped in the dumpster out back and mixed around with other trash from the hotel. The trash pickup hadn't come yet, though."

"This is very interesting," Deloris said appreciatively. Then she mused aloud. "So, David must have eaten something at the restaurant that made him sick. But how would anyone be able to give him arsenic unless someone slipped into the kitchen? And what about Dr. Browne? Could he have slipped into the kitchen to poison David's food, or did he give him something earlier that made him sick with a delayed reaction? But then arsenic takes about thirty minutes to react, and the food was served two hours before David left sick. Surely, someone in the kitchen would have noticed someone out of place messing with the food. Then what about Dr. Johnson? Same problem as Dr. Browne. Someone would have seen him in the kitchen if he had been there."

Both the waiter and George agreed with what Deloris deduced. The waiter said that the cook runs a tight ship and no one, but no one, was allowed in the kitchen during prep time. That ruled out any outside person being in the kitchen.

"Do you remember what Dr. Kerns had to eat and drink?" Deloris asked.

He replied, "They both had filet mignon, baked potato, green beans, and coffee. Lots of coffee."

Deloris wrote all this down in her notepad. "Okay, thank

you very much, Ralph. You've been a great help."

"I hope you get all of this resolved, because people are hesitant to eat at our restaurant," Ralph said with a look of concern on his face. "The attendance has been down significantly since David's death. I rely on tips to make ends meet, and no customers mean no tips."

"I'll do my best to find the source of the poison," Deloris said calmly. "I'm pretty sure the restaurant is not to blame since the timing is off."

Ralph had a look of relief on his face and thanked her by shaking her hand energetically.

She and George headed back to the elevator when George pointed out the house peeper and suggested that they should talk with him.

Deloris followed his pointed finger to see a man about sixty years old wearing a wrinkled gray suit that barely buttoned across his wide girth. The white shirt he wore under the suit jacket was also wrinkled, with a few stains on it. His red tie was slightly askew. On his head was a gray fedora with a black band, slightly cocked to one side. He had the look of a seasoned, grizzly detective.

Deloris said, "The who?"

"The house peeper, you know. The house dick," George replied.

"Oh yes, the house detective. We should talk to him. Was he one of the security staff called to check on David when he was found dead?"

"Yes. He must have been since we only have one house dick and he keeps a room in the hotel," George replied.

"Yes, we definitely should talk with him then," Deloris agreed.

As they approached the detective, he eyed George suspiciously and growled, "What do you want, genius? I don't have time to mess with you, you little pipsqueak."

Well, it was obvious the guy didn't like George. Deloris tried her luck and stepped in front of George to ask, "Are you the detective who found Dr. David Kerns's body on Valentine's Day?"

His face softened a little. "Yeah, whose skirt, are you?"

George took that as a clue and said, "Elbert Floyd, this is Deloris Markham, my..." Deloris stepped on his foot, stopping him before he finished the sentence. He looked at her, and she cautiously shook her head no.

Deloris didn't want George to tell him anything about their relationship so that Detective Floyd would take her seriously and not connect her to his interactions with George. She quickly added, "Sorry, George." Turning to the detective, she said, "I'm a friend, or I was a friend of Dr. David Kerns, and I work at the Kansas City Police Department. I'm helping my colleagues, Detectives Austin Martin and Jim Anderson, with their investigation. We are trying to find out everything we can about what happened to the deceased."

The officer replied, "Well, go talk with your colleagues then. I can't tell you anything more than what you read in the newspapers." And with that, he walked past them, giving George the evil eye as he passed.

"Rats. We don't know diddly squat from that conversation," Deloris lamented.

Having gone through the remaining hotel staff list, she said goodbye to George, saying they would talk later. He attempted to plant a kiss on her face, but she dodged his advances.

"Ah, sugar, don't be that way," George pleaded.

"Don't think you can cheat on me and then come back to be sweet on me," she told him. She had no intention of kissing him right now, anyway. He could have his little girlfriend at the front desk for all she cared, but she didn't want to let him know she didn't care. He needed to learn how to treat a woman properly.

Chapter Thirteen
Intruder

Friday night, when Deloris got home from The Ship at two in the morning, she tiptoed into the house to keep from waking anyone up. She got up to her room, turned on the light, and screamed. It had been ransacked! The window was open, and the room was so cold she could see her breath. The dresser drawers had all been pulled out, the sheets on the bed were stripped, and the mattress had been turned over. Everything was in shambles. Even her rug was askew, but it still covered most of her hiding place, which looked untouched.

Her scream brought all the boarders and Thelma to her room. Annie, terrified but ready to fight, was carrying an iron that she used as a doorstop. Gracie arrived carrying a chair. Her hair was tied up in rags, making her look like Little Orphan Annie's friend, but tomorrow her hair would look glamorous with long curls. Leota showed up in a mud facemask with her hairbrush in hand. Cecilia slept through the commotion because her bedroom was on the first floor at the back of the house. Thelma, with her mother's hearing, came running up the stairs with a poker from the fireplace. Her hair was twisted in small spit curls; each held together with two bobby pins crisscrossed and a hairnet to hold them all in. Tomorrow, her head would be covered in small curls, looking as if she had a perm. She obviously put her glasses on in a rush, because one earpiece wasn't completely down on her ear, making the glasses askew on her face.

Deloris, looking at her rescuers with their various weapons and different levels of wakefulness, had to laugh, saying that any thief had better watch out in their house because they made quite a scary sight.

Thelma closed the window, and then they all left Deloris's room to go check the rest of the house and make sure the intruder was gone. Deloris closed the door after them and checked under her bed to confirm that her bag was still safely secured in its hiding place. Confident nothing was missing; she went downstairs to call the police switchboard. She knew the number, but was used to answering calls, not making them. One by one, her housemates came to her while she was on the phone and reported that no one had been found in the house. Since the intruder was obviously gone, the dispatcher said they would send an officer to drive by the house and through the neighborhood to see if anyone was lurking about. Otherwise, an officer would be sent by the house later in the morning for a report. Deloris agreed and hung up.

Satisfied that the house was secure, everyone eventually got back to sleep for the few morning hours left to sleep. It took a while for Deloris to fall asleep. Who in the world was in her room, and why didn't anyone else hear them break-in? They had to be there for a while to disturb so many things in her room. Having an intruder in her room left her uneasy and feeling slightly vulnerable. When she finally turned out the light, she couldn't shut her brain off from running through the list of murder suspects, so she turned the light back on and wrote them down:

Bob Scott

Lucy McCoy

Dr. Jeremiah Browne

Dr. Donald Johnson

Mysterious intruder

But first, who was the intruder? Were they one and the same person, as the murderer? It was a good thing she didn't have to work at the switchboard tomorrow, because she was worn out. She turned out the light again and decided that she would ask Austin to investigate it, too.

The next morning, she woke up to a light knocking on her door.

"DeDe, the police are here to follow-up on the intruder last night." It was Thelma.

"I'll be down in a jiffy," Deloris responded, rubbing her eyes.

She was disappointed that neither Austin nor Big Jim was sent, but then she realized it was Saturday and they would have some time off from the department. The officer took her name and asked, "Is anything missing?" Nothing that she could find, she replied. She showed him her bedroom and described the state it had been in. He glanced around, made a few notes, and they returned to the downstairs entryway. As he handed her a copy of the account, he said, "Thank you, Miss Markham. We'll be in touch if we find out who did it, but I should tell you that since nothing was taken, it won't be a very high priority. If you could come down to the station to make a more formal report, I'd appreciate it."

"I do understand, Officer. Thank you for coming to take my statement. I'll stop by and do that." And Deloris bid him goodbye.

Later that day, Deloris went to the police department and

asked to talk with Austin, on the chance he would be at work on a Saturday. Joey was working the front desk and was very professional in his response to Deloris. She figured he must have received a reprimand from the other day when she tricked him into leaving the front desk.

"Hello, Miss Markham. Austin isn't here today, but his partner, Big Jim, is. If you'll please wait here, I'll let him know you are here." He turned stiffly to the phone and called back to Big Jim, who then came to the desk.

"What brings you in on a Saturday, Deloris?" he asked.

She told him about her room having been ransacked. Then she told him what she had learned from Bob Scott the night before, omitting her new plan to go to David Kerns's house and interview the neighbors. She figured Big Jim would try to talk her out of doing that, so she wouldn't tell him about it.

While they were talking, Austin walked in.

"What are you doing here? Joey said you weren't working today," Deloris asked, surprised to see him.

"This case on David has me bothered, and I couldn't sleep last night so I decided to come in and work on it." Austin replied.

"Since you're here, I need to tell you what happened last night." She relayed to him everything she had told Big Jim.

"We need to get you a gun so you can protect yourself. You can borrow my revolver. It's a snub-nosed .38," Austin offered.

"I don't know how to use a gun," Deloris said apologetically.

"How about we go out to the country so you can learn how to use it and get a little target practice in?" Austin offered.

“I won’t have time until next week. I’m working a double shift at The Ship on Saturday and helping the Indiana Gardens restaurant with a special event on Sunday,” Deloris said.

“That’s okay. We’ll find a day next week,” Austin agreed. “Here, you take it until then.”

“Are you sure that I should take it?” she questioned, looking at Big Jim for his input.

He nodded and said, “I agree with Austin. You need to protect yourself if you are going to keep inserting yourself into police business.” Deloris groaned at the last part.

“Yes, I want you to have protection, whether or not you know how to use it yet,” Austin encouraged.

“I guess I can do that,” Deloris relented as she took the gun from him.

He showed her how to hold the gun safely and how to load it. Then he showed her how to unload it and to make sure it was unloaded before pointing at anything or anyone she didn’t want to shoot.

She gingerly put the gun in her purse and thanked him.

When she got home, she found a dozen roses sitting in the middle of the dining room table. There was a note from George apologizing. She breathed in their fragrance and smiled. It was good for George to learn not to take her for granted. The telephone rang, and she rushed to answer it. George was on the other end.

“Did the flowers arrive?” he asked.

“Yes, they did, and they are lovely. Thank you,” she replied softly.

"I'm sorry for hurting you," he apologized.

She said, "Well, don't do it again, okay?"

"I won't," he replied. "How about a date tomorrow night?"

She accepted his apology, and they planned to go out.

Chapter Fourteen

The Funeral

The coroner finally released David's body to the funeral home for burial on Monday. Deloris asked Mary Virginia for time off from the switchboard to help David's mother make funeral arrangements and then to attend the funeral. Mary Virginia told her there was no problem and not to worry about it.

Deloris felt she needed to see if Mrs. Kerns needed any help to plan his funeral. She would offer to help her, but then set up a time later to come visit with her. She really wanted to know what her letter said and try to find other clues that might be in her house. When her shift was over, she took a bus to Mrs. Kerns's house on Ward Parkway.

From the street, Deloris looked up at Blanche Kerns's grand Italian Renaissance-style home with its brick-red tube tile roof crowning the limestone exterior. At the sidewalk, two masonry lions guarded either side of the five steps leading up the path that ended at the front door. The pathway was lined with shrubbery, dormant now in the winter. There were remnants of flowers and ground cover filling in the gaps in the stepping-stone edging from when the plants were alive that summer. None of their beauty was left in the cold, harsh Kansas City winter. In the front yard, on one side, was a birdbath with a circle of dead flowers, and a trellis covered in dormant vines was on the other side. The portico with its four columns provided shelter from the weather around the front door. Long windows were inset on either side of the front door. Three shorter windows, evenly spaced, were above the entrance on the second floor. The style and spacing of the windows on the front were repeated on both sides of the house.

Deloris walked up four steps to the front door and raised the heavy knocker, hitting the door with it three times. She assumed that the older woman who answered the door was Esther Hernandez, Mrs. Kerns's maid, based on what David had told her about Esther. David had also told her about Esther's brother, Jose Gomez, who worked for his mother as well as a gardener, landscaper, and chauffeur.

"May I help you?" Esther asked, looking at Deloris suspiciously.

"Hello, my name is Deloris Markham, and I've come to see Mrs. Kerns. I want to offer her my condolences and ask if she needs my help planning David's funeral. I was a close friend of her son."

"Come in and wait here, please," she said as she closed the door behind Deloris. Esther had kind eyes, but years of sadness were behind them.

Inside the entryway, Deloris stood, looking around after Esther went into a room on the right and closed the door. A large chandelier hung in the middle of the room over a round, dark mahogany table. Underneath it was a small Persian rug with muted red and gold colors. Behind the table was a dark mahogany staircase with large, heavy newel posts that had lion heads carved into the wood. A red brick fireplace trimmed in dark mahogany was on the left. A small, dark mahogany table was on the right side of the room, opposite the fireplace, and had a chair pulled up beside it. On the table sat a black candlestick telephone, with a pad of paper and a pen next to it. The dark wood floors and dim lights gave the atmosphere of doom and gloom, giving Deloris the chills. The house felt more like a mausoleum or funeral parlor than a home.

She could hear Mrs. Kerns and Esther talking behind the door. Then Esther returned and said, "I'm sorry, but Mrs. Kerns isn't feeling very well today and asked that you come back later."

"Yes, I understand. Tell her she can contact me later when she feels better. Here is my telephone number." Deloris ran to the pad of paper by the telephone. Before she wrote on it, she tore the top sheet off and deftly put it in her pocket. She didn't know if it would provide any useful information, but figured she'd take it just in case. She jotted down her name and telephone number and handed it to Esther, then exited the intimidating house.

When Deloris got home, she took the first sheet of paper from Mrs. Kerns's house and placed it on the table. She lightly shaded it with her pencil. She could just make out the numbers on it, but it looked like it was Dr. Browne's telephone number. So she threw it away.

Deloris never received a call from Mrs. Kerns. She assumed that someone else had helped her with the funeral arrangements, but she still wanted to talk with her about her letter and find out if there were any more clues in her house.

While the funeral was to be in Kansas City, the burial would be at a later date in the old Hickory Creek Cemetery outside of Jameson. The ground was too frozen to bury anyone in February, so it was common practice for funeral homes to keep bodies on ice and wait until spring to complete the burial.

A few days later, on the day of the funeral, she was in her room getting ready, and a thought came to her. She had read somewhere that murderers sometimes attended the funerals of their victims to see where the investigations were leading and if they were under suspicion. With that in mind, she would observe which of the suspects attended the funeral and acted suspiciously.

In a small chapel at the funeral home, Dr. David Kerns lay in repose. White milk glass vases were on either side of the casket and held snowdrops and daffodils. An organist played "The Old Rugged Cross" softly from the next room. Deloris approached to offer her sympathy to Mrs. Kerns, who sat at the front of the room. Esther sat behind her and nodded to Deloris in acknowledgement. Deloris was shocked to see Mrs. Kerns. This woman always took great care of her looks, starched and pressed, looking like a million dollars. Today, she looked like death warmed over, dressed in black with a black lace scarf covering her head. Deloris could see that her silver-gray hair wasn't carefully coiffed under the scarf, as it usually was, and her lipstick was a little lopsided, not carefully applied. She had lost weight, and her eyes were sunken with dark circles under them. It was obvious the entire ordeal had taken its toll on her and her health. Deloris never really cared for Mrs. Kerns because she was always rude and snobby to her, but today she felt sorry for her. She looked so small, frail, and old.

Mrs. Kerns didn't recognize Deloris at first, but when she identified herself, she said, "Oh yes, of course. Deloris, how are you? I'm sorry I didn't call you back. I've just felt so rough these last few days. David told me..." and her voice caught a little at mentioning his name. Regaining her composure, she continued, "David told me you two often met for lunch."

"Yes, we met almost every Thursday for lunch."

Deloris told Mrs. Kerns how very sorry she was for her loss and that David had given her his father's pocket watch to be repaired (a little lie) and she wanted to give it back to Mrs. Kerns.

"Oh yes, bless you, my child."

"May I come by your house tomorrow afternoon at about one o'clock to return it?"

Mrs. Kerns agreed, and Deloris walked up to the casket, but she couldn't bring herself to look in. She wanted to remember David as the vibrant, healthy man he was in life. She took a seat at the back of the chapel to watch who would come and go. It wasn't long before Austin and Big Jim arrived. Taking off their hats as they entered the chapel, they spotted Deloris and took seats next to her. They apparently had the same idea.

Next to arrive was Dr. Jeremiah Browne, David's business partner. He walked up to Mrs. Kerns, held her hand, and said a few words to her. He then walked up to the coffin and stood there for an extended time before leaving the building.

Several older people whom Deloris didn't know but who were very well dressed and seemed to be dripping in money arrived. They talked with Mrs. Kerns, holding up the line. She assumed they were some of Mrs. Kerns's high-society friends.

Deloris turned to see Thelma and the girls walk in and gave them a slight wave in acknowledgement. Behind them were Roy Markham, Deloris's oldest brother, and Clarence. They must have driven down from up home, as did a few other people Deloris recognized. After offering their condolences to Mrs. Kerns, they sat directly in front of Deloris, Austin, and Big Jim.

Dorothy Braxton, along with other employees and the president of the Jameson Farmer's Bank, walked in next. When Dorothy saw Deloris, she gave her a deathly glare that could have melted ice. She must have realized that David was dead when Deloris was up there and she duped her into opening the safe deposit box. "She'll get over it," Deloris thought.

Leota Jones came in next. She was a blubbering mess with a yellow daisy-flowered handkerchief in hand, and when she looked at David in the coffin, she let out a wail and went running out of the chapel.

Dr. Myron Cramer entered next with a somber look on his face. He walked up to Mrs. Kerns, kneeled down, took her hand, and spoke a few words to her. He then approached the coffin and lowered his head, shaking it slowly as if in disbelief. He took a seat on the left, in the middle row.

Bob Scott and Lucy McCoy entered next, but you could hear them before you saw them because Lucy was wailing loudly in the hallway. Bob had to hold her up as they walked toward the front. She approached Mrs. Kerns, but Mrs. Kerns turned her head the other way. Lucy stood there for a minute, not initially realizing the snub. Finally, she awkwardly turned to walk toward the coffin. Standing in front of it, she grabbed David's hand, saying, "Oh, David! Why, oh why, did you do this to me?" She put his hand on her heart, and the funeral director had to intervene before she pulled the corpse out of the casket. Bob took her hand and quickly guided her to a seat towards the front. She put on quite a grandiose act for all to see.

Standing at the back, but not truly entering the chapel, was a man who covertly had his hat pulled low over his face. He was tall and slender, with graying temples. He stood staring at the coffin with a slight smirk on his face, then he turned and left. Deloris recognized him from his military gait. It was Dr. Donald Johnson! As he started walking out of the doorway, he almost collided with Annie, but hurried off without an apology. Startled, Annie turned to watch his departure. Big Jim stood up and motioned to an officer stationed at the door, and the officer left. Another officer stepped up and took his place at the door.

Annie was walking in with Gracie, Carol, and Deloris's neighbors, Evie and Nora Davis, who were followed by their parents, Ben and Charlotte Davis. The group walked down to Mrs. Kerns and then to the coffin together. All of them had been patients of Dr. Kerns, and grief was etched upon their faces.

Just before the service started, Jose Gomez, Mrs. Kerns's gardener, and Dominic Marini, the local butcher, walked in. They quickly took seats next to Esther, behind Mrs. Kerns.

The preacher gave a nice eulogy. It helped to make the service much more personal since he had been a patient of Dr. Kerns since Dr. Walters' death. A singer in the room with the organist sang a religious song, "I Go to the Garden Alone," and then the funeral director escorted Mrs. Kerns out of the room, followed by Esther, Jose, and Dominic.

Deloris, Austin, and Big Jim lingered inside the funeral home after the service. Roy and Clarence walked up to the group, and Thelma joined them.

"Are you heading back home now?" Thelma asked her brothers. "I was hoping you could stay and have a meal with us."

"Yes, you know we need to get back up there to do our chores. The horses and cattle can't feed themselves," Clarence answered.

"Tell Momma I'll be sending her a letter soon, but I've been a little busy. Tell her and Dad, I love them," Deloris said, looking remorseful that they weren't staying.

"From me, too," Thelma added.

"We will," Clarence turned to Austin and shook his hand, as did Roy. Austin quickly introduced them to Big Jim, and they shook hands. Thelma said her goodbyes to the group and walked outside with Clarence and Roy. Her girls followed.

Once they had left, Deloris offered to give Big Jim and Austin her observations from the funeral if they would tell her what they had found out from Bob Scott and Lucy McCoy. First, she asked if they knew who the fellow was standing in the back but never walked into the chapel.

Big Jim replied, "No, but I assume you must be talking about the mysterious, elusive Dr. Donald Johnson."

"You are correct. I recognized him from the way he walked, even though he tried to hide his face with his hat pulled so low."

Big Jim said, "I only saw him for a moment and then he was gone, but his quick exit made me suspicious, so I had the officer watching the entrance pick the guy up and take him to the station."

Deloris added, "I'm not surprised he didn't come in and take a seat after everything he has done to both David and Dr. Cramer. Did you see a slight smile or a smirk on his face? It made him look like the evil Doctor Gorham in the scary movie from a few years ago, Murders at the Zoo."

"No, I missed that," Austin replied. "Well, that alone must mean he is guilty. Right?"

"Oh, you," Deloris gave him a slight punch on the arm. "I'm serious. But did you also see how he rushed off?"

"Yeah, that's why Jim sent the officer after him, remember?" Austin said sarcastically, and Deloris groaned.

Annie walked up to the group and said, "Hey, do you guys know who the fellow was that almost knocked me down? He was so rude and never even said he was sorry. He just kept on moving."

"Yes, that was Dr. Johnson, one of the suspects," Deloris told her.

"Well, that figures," Annie said. "He's guilty in my book from that encounter alone."

"It doesn't surprise me; he would do that, given what we know about his demeanor. From what I've heard from Dr. Cramer, he is a vulgar, self-serving person," Deloris shared.

"I hope you catch him and that he is the culprit. I can't wait to write about him in the newspaper," Annie said with a wink. "I need to get back to work. I'll see you later, DeDe."

"Bye." Deloris then turned to Austin and Big Jim and said, "So, what can you tell me about your interview with Dr. Cramer?"

"You'll be pleased to know that Dr. Cramer corroborated everything you told us about Johnson."

"Of course he did. I didn't lie," Deloris felt a little irritated, but continued, “I remember David mentioning him briefly. I almost forgot to tell you that when he went for the interview, he told me one of the secretaries handed him an envelope with a note telling him he had better leave or else. At the time, he said that he had thrown the note away and laughed about it with Dr. Cramer when they met.”

Deloris asked Austin and Big Jim if she could catch a ride with them. They continued talking about the case, and she finally remembered to tell them about the contents of the safe deposit box and the ring. Something dawned on her as she talked: “Could that be what Lucy or the person was looking for when they ransacked my room?”

“Why would she think you would have the ring?” Austin asked her suspiciously.

“Who knows what she or whoever would think? They know I was David’s friend and he could have given it to me for safekeeping,” Deloris defended her statement.

“We’ll take it under consideration,” Austin accepted her suggestion.

When they arrived at Thelma’s, Deloris hopped out of the car and thanked Big Jim for the ride. She had a date with George that evening and needed to get ready.

George picked her up in his brother’s car, a 1929 Ford Model A Tudor Sedan.

“Holy smoke. You look like a million dollars,” he said as he held the car door open for her.

To make up for Valentine’s Day, he took her out to eat at Italian Gardens Restaurant, a restaurant often confused with Indiana Gardens Restaurant, where she occasionally worked.

After the meal, they went to the Uptown Theater to watch Don't Get Personal with James Dunn and Sally Eilers. Even though it was her kind of movie, with the Bad Girl Team, as they called themselves, Deloris couldn't take her mind off the mystery surrounding David Kerns. She tried to focus on the movie and show George her appreciation for all his efforts, but she couldn't wait to get home.

When he pulled the car in front of the boardinghouse, she said, "Thank you, Georgie. This has all been very nice. A suitable replacement for Valentine's Day. I love the roses, and the meal was wonderful. The movie was my favorite kind of movie. I truly appreciate all of your efforts to make this evening very special."

His chest swelled with pride, and she let him kiss her. She then explained to him that she was a little tired and needed to go. Disappointed, he understood, and she got out of the car.

In her room, she pulled out her new Big Chief writing tablet that Thelma had bought her for Christmas. The writing tablet was too large for her to take with her when she was gathering clues, but she didn't want to tell Thelma. She went over all the suspects and the information she had so far. Nothing else jumped out at her. Lying there awake, she thought about Lucy. Maybe she was the one who broke into her room and ransacked it looking for the ring. But how did she do that with no one seeing or hearing her? How would she know Deloris had the ring? "The puzzle pieces just aren't fitting together properly," she said to herself as she finally drifted off to sleep.

Chapter Fifteen

Mrs. Kerns

Deloris awoke with a start when she heard a car backfire on the street. It startled her, especially after last Friday night's experience with the intruder. She could smell bacon cooking and, yes, coffee. She needed some coffee to get her day started. Today, she would visit Mrs. Kerns and take her the watch when she got off work at the switchboard. Deloris threw the covers back, put on her slippers, and grabbed her robe. Leota was in the bathroom, so she had to wait; however, there was always the old outhouse in the backyard if Leota took too long. That was always the last resort. Oh good, Leota opened the door, and Deloris rushed past her. Leota yelled, "Watch out!" and turned to give her a glare. Deloris didn't care because she needed to get into the bathroom and couldn't wait to be polite. She noticed that Leota still looked a little peaked with dark circles under her eyes, but she had obviously felt well enough to go to work the past week and to watch the girls. The medicine Dr. Browne gave her must have worked.

When Deloris went downstairs, Annie and Cecilia were eating their breakfast, and Leota was just sitting down to eat hers. Gracie was already at the coroner's office. Thelma was in the kitchen washing up from the first wave of breakfast dishes. She and her daughters ate breakfast first, then Annie, Cecilia, and Gracie were the second shift, with Deloris and Leota the third shift. Thelma went to her bedroom to catch a few hours of shuteye before she had to leave for her weekday lunch shift at the diner. So, Deloris had to cook her own eggs. Because Thelma also worked at the egg factory Sundays through Thursdays, she got to bring home eggs that were slightly cracked or rejects. The free eggs helped the weekly food budget.

After breakfast, Deloris went to her room and retrieved David's watch from the canvas bag, then she left for work. Before she went upstairs to the switchboard, she stopped in to talk with Austin and Big Jim for a minute. Big Jim was there, but Austin was in the evidence room. She brought up her room being ransacked the week before.

"The more I think about it, the more I believe Lucy could have ransacked my room," she said.

"It's possible," Big Jim replied. "Anyway, we plan to arrest Lucy on an outstanding warrant we found on her for stealing from Pecks' Store. We'll see if we can get her to confess to that as well," he chuckled a little.

"I plan to see Mrs. Kerns later this afternoon, and then I plan to go to David's house tomorrow or Saturday and maybe interview the neighbors."

"You need to be careful," Big Jim warned.

While they were talking, Austin walked in. "Hey DeDe. What brings you down here to see us?"

She filled him in on Lucy probably being the one who ransacked her room. Then she asked, "Hey, what did you find out when you talked with Dr. Johnson? And did Dr. Cramer say anything new?"

"We asked Cramer again about the night he met with David to see if there was anything new to add, but other than the time he met with David at 7:00 p.m. and he seemed distracted, there wasn't anything new. He said that David was a solid guy and he would help us any way he could to find out who did this," Big Jim reported.

"Is there anything else?" Deloris pressed.

"Well, I probably shouldn't tell you this, but Lucy McCoy and Bob Scott both have rap sheets," Austin divulged. "Bob's rap sheet was for assault and battery, and Lucy's was for stealing. In the meantime, Dr. Browne is expected to come back into the precinct tomorrow, as is Bob Scott."

"Yes, Big Jim mentioned Lucy had an outstanding warrant. What about Dr. Johnson?" Deloris persisted.

"We asked him where he was on the evening of the 13th, and he told us he was having dinner with his wife at the Savoy Grill. They went to a movie afterwards before returning to the hotel and bed," Austin shared.

"Did you ask him which movie?" Deloris asked eagerly.

"They caught a taxi and saw Times Square Lady at the La Salle Theater at Broadway and Armour. We found the taxi driver, and he corroborated his story," Austin replied.

"What about after the movie?" Deloris continued.

Austin sighed. "Yes, we checked with the desk clerk on duty that night, and he said he saw Dr. Johnson slip out of the hotel about 10 p.m. So, we are going to bring him in for more questioning in the morning."

Then she said, "He? It wasn't a girl?"

"No, they said a man worked the front desk at night, so we talked to him," Big Jim answered.

"Oh, that makes sense. A girl named Ann Green works there in the afternoons and early evenings, and I talked with her."

"Oh really? What did she have to say?" Austin asked.

"She told me Lucy went to the hotel to see David twice. One time when he first arrived at the hotel to meet Dr. Cramer, and a second time around nine o'clock. David wouldn't talk with Lucy and brushed her off. The elevator operator told me that David and Dr. Johnson had an argument in the elevator." She waited for their reaction before proceeding. "I never got to talk to the maid, Aline or Alley Cat, they call her, but I plan to keep looking for her."

"We can look for her," Austin quickly jumped in. "That's our job, remember?"

"Okay. I think she lives somewhere near Strawberry Hill. Anyway, I really appreciate you giving me an update," Deloris said with sincerity.

"Man, I feel like I just gave a report to Chief Douglas," Austin chuckled and looked at Big Jim.

Big Jim laughed and said, "I know. Hey, I need to get this report to the Chief. I'll see you later, Deloris. Thanks for the information." He walked away, still chuckling and shaking his head.

Deloris was lost in thought and missed the joke. Austin cleared his throat to regain her attention. "We need to schedule target practice with the gun, Deloris. How about doing it after you see Mrs. Kerns? You should know what you are doing if you're going to go poking around in murders."

"I don't know how long I will spend with Mrs. Kerns, though. If it gets too late, can we do it tomorrow or this weekend?"

Deloris asked.

"Sure, we can, kiddo," Austin agreed.

"I'm not a kiddo," Deloris protested.

"You are to me," Austin countered. "You're younger than me, remember." He then hurried away before Deloris could say anything else, leaving her standing there with a frustrated look. He seldom succeeded in getting the last word in, but he did today as he walked away with a big grin on his face.

With a snarl, Deloris went upstairs to the switchboard. At the end of her shift, she clocked out and ran downstairs but didn't see either detective. She hoped to talk Austin into giving her a ride to Mrs. Kerns's house, but took a taxi instead. Hailing a taxi was a little extravagant, but she still had some of the money left from the stash Willie and Mr. Corbane gave her. Funny that David lived as far away as he could from his mother and still be in the same city, she noted when she compared his address to his mother's. She remembered him saying that his mother drove him crazy with her highfalutin ways. "You can take a boy out of the country, but you can't take the country out of the boy," he would say with a wink and a laugh.

Knocking on Mrs. Kerns's door, Deloris took a moment to look around the neighborhood. The front of Mrs. Kerns's estate faced Ward Parkway. It was in a very high-class area with close proximity to the Plaza, a fairly new upscale shopping area in south Kansas City. Esther came to the door and let Deloris inside. She led Deloris into the parlor, where Mrs. Kerns was seated crocheting what looked like a lap robe.

Deloris took her coat and headscarf off and placed them on the sofa with her purse. As she took a seat on the sofa,

Mrs. Kerns asked about Deloris' parents and how they were. Deloris was surprised at her question because she didn't think Mrs. Kerns even knew her parents. Then she asked how Deloris had been and where she was living now. Deloris had never seen her so kind and gracious before. The shock of losing David must have really affected her.

Deloris told her about living with Thelma and her little girls. She also told her about the other boarders: Annie, Gracie, Cecilia, and Leota. She told Mrs. Kerns about how she enjoyed spending her lunches with David and how much she was going to miss him.

After pleasantries, Deloris said, "I brought you this," and handed Mrs. Kerns the pocket watch. Tears welled up in the elderly lady's eyes. After a moment or two, Mrs. Kerns said that she didn't know what she was going to do with it now that David was gone and she didn't have any other close relatives to give it to. She had relatives in California, but they didn't really know her husband or David very well. Did Deloris have someone she would like to give it to? Deloris said that she was certain her brother Roy would be honored to have it, since he and David had been such good friends in school. Or if not him, maybe her brother Clarence might be honored to have it, since he worked for her husband and thought highly of him. Mrs. Kerns handed her the pocket watch and told her to give it to either of them. Deloris thanked her and put it back in her purse.

"Since I don't have any close relatives, I'm leaving my entire estate and money to fund a Christian medical mission overseas that my doctor told me about," Mrs. Kerns revealed.

"That sounds like a noble cause," Deloris said gently. "Who is your doctor?"

"Dr. Jeremiah Browne," she said. "I used to go to Dr. Walters, but he passed away." A sad look crossed her face and her shoulders slumped a little. She looked down slowly, shaking her head, and sniffled into her handkerchief.

"I'm so sorry," Deloris sympathized. "My sister went to Dr. Walters. He delivered both of her babies. I understand he was a great doctor."

"He was, but I only went to him for a short time before he passed and my David took his place, you know."

"Yes, David told me about that." Deloris shifted in her seat. "I actually have a question for you, Mrs. Kerns. I understand you received a letter from David. I received one, too. Would you mind telling me what your letter said?"

"It said that I needed to help you with anything you might need. I have the letter here." She reached for an envelope that was on the table next to her.

Deloris took the one letter from the older woman and looked it over. Mrs. Kerns said, "I'm uncertain in what way I can help you, but please let me know what you need and I will do what I can."

Inspired by this revelation, Deloris thought about the end of David's letter and asked Mrs. Kerns if she knew anything about an hourglass. For a moment, Mrs. Kerns stared at her in disbelief, perhaps, but then she took her cane and slowly rose from her seat. She went to an old drop-front secretary bookcase in the corner of the room that was filled with books. Mrs. Kerns produced a key that hung from her watch chain and unlocked the front to reveal a desk with nooks to hold letters, bills, and various other papers. A fountain pen and a bottle of ink were on one side. Under the nook was a space wide enough to store larger items, and it was from there that Mrs. Kerns gently pulled out an old book called The Hourglass. Deloris could see that it was old and fragile, so she took it gingerly from Mrs. Kerns. An envelope was sticking out of the book, and Deloris pulled it out to hand it to Mrs. Kerns. She noticed that the address on the envelope was from someone in California.

Mrs. Kerns said, "Now how did that get in there? Sorry, dear, that is a letter from a distant cousin of mine. I haven't heard from her since my husband died. It has probably been five years since she wrote. I must have used the envelope as a bookmark and never took it out."

In the back of the book was a second envelope that had Deloris's name on it, so she opened it. Inside was a copy of David's will that was dated one week before he died. In it, he named Deloris as his sole heir and the recipient of the stock certificates and all contents she had found earlier in his safe deposit box. She was also to inherit his bank account, his house, car, and jewelry. That must be why he put the key to his house in the safe-deposit box. Deloris was stunned. She didn't know what to think. For the first time in her life, she was speechless. She sat down on the settee and looked at Mrs. Kerns, who was crying as she nodded in affirmation.

"I, I don't understand," Deloris stammered. "He wanted me to have everything? What about you?" Deloris was in a state of shock.

Mrs. Kerns said between sobs, "Yes, dear, he thought very highly of you. I have everything I need here." Deloris put her arm around Mrs. Kerns's shoulders, which were shaking with each sob, and they cried together. Deloris had never seen Mrs. Kerns so kind and loving. If only she would show this side of herself more often.

Deloris only stayed a little while longer because Mrs. Kerns looked exhausted. When she felt it was appropriate to leave, she did so and returned home in a state of shock. Her first thought was that David must have realized he was going to die soon, but how? Why? Unless it truly was a suicide. “Oh, David, what was going on with you?”

In the cab on the way home, she ruminated about his life and wondered what in the world had brought him to this stage? David was so successful and popular among his patients and, really, everyone. He had everything except a wife and family with whom he could share it all. Then the realization set in that she was now a homeowner. She remembered David telling her about the seven-bedroom, three-bathroom house with a carriage house behind it when he bought it. At the time when he told her about it, she thought it seemed an enormous house for just him.

“Just imagine what Thelma will think when I tell her we have a new house to move into?!” Deloris thought. Then another realization came to her. What in the world was she going to do with a car? Watching the driver as he navigated through the city, she feared she couldn’t drive one of these infernal contraptions to save her soul. There were too many levers, knobs, and pedals for her to master. That was one puzzle she couldn’t crack.

Chapter Sixteen

Target Practice

Yesterday, when Deloris had told everyone the news at Thelma's house about her inheritance, Leota screamed at her, "Well, you finally got what you wanted out of David, didn't you?" She looked square at Deloris and added, "You always get everything your way!" Then she ran to her room in a flood of tears. Deloris had never seen this side of Leota before. There was pure hatred on her face. Everyone else was also shocked at her outburst. After a moment of stunned silence, they turned to Deloris and congratulated her in excited voices.

Later, Deloris went to her room and put the will and pocket watch in her canvas bag. Then she stopped with an envelope in hand when she realized she hadn't opened the additional letter Mrs. Kerns had given her. She reached for her letter opener, which she kept in her side table drawer that also served as a weapon if needed. Unfolding the letter, she began to read.

Dear Deloris,

If you're reading this letter, then I must be dead. I'm sorry for being so cryptic with everything, but I think I am being poisoned, and I don't know who is trying to kill me. If anyone can figure out this puzzle, I'm certain you can. I am also sorry for not telling you sooner, but I needed to be sure before I said anything. I didn't want my letters with clues to fall into the wrong hands, so I made them as innocuous as I could, hoping you'd understand. I have a safe at my house, and I know you will know what to do with it. I've always admired you for your kind heart and ability to solve crimes. You have the tenacity to see justice served, so I know you can sort this mystery out. I hope you enjoy living in my house and driving my car. Yes, I know you can't drive, but now you have an incentive to learn. I am giving you all of my worldly goods because I want you to be able to continue your mission to do good for others and not worry about where the finances would come from to do so. I also want you to be comfortable. You have been a good friend and so kind to listen to my rants. Please give my regards to your parents, family, and Austin. Tell Roy I tried.

In kindest regards,

David

She read the letter again before going to work. With tears in her eyes, she sat on her bed to think about everything David had said in his letter. After a short while, she went downstairs. Annie was there, just finishing her breakfast.

"Annie, I'm going to David's house later today. Will you go with me and help me search for clues?" Deloris asked.

"I'll be there," Annie replied. They worked out an approximate time, and Annie went upstairs to finish getting ready for work.

Looking at the time, Deloris rushed back to her room because she needed to catch a bus to the police station. She wasn't sure she wanted to tell Joyce, Pam, Lori, and Julie about her inheritance---at least not yet. She couldn't find her headscarf; where'd she put it? She looked everywhere, then realized that she must have left it at Mrs. Kerns's house. Well, she'd go back to see her this weekend and get it. She needed to leave the house now, or she would be late. She grabbed her purse and coat to run out the door, but her purse opened and the contents spilled out. As she was gathering everything, she realized she had forgotten to put Austin's gun in her purse. She moved the rug and pulled her bag out of its hiding place under her bed. She quickly pulled the gun out of the bag and slipped it into her purse. Returning the bag to the floor hiding space, she replaced the floor slats and pulled the rug over them. She then flew downstairs in a rush and ran all the way down the block to the bus stop. "If only I could drive David's car, now would be a good time to use it," she thought. Topping the hill with the bus stop in view, she saw the bus pulling away. Out of breath and out of luck, she stopped running. She went through the options in her head. Everyone at Thelma's was at work already, and Thelma couldn't drive either, so she'd have to return to the boardinghouse and call a taxi.

When Deloris walked in at the switchboard, everyone started teasing her for being fifteen minutes late. She put her coat and purse away and walked to Mary Virginia's office to apologize.

"I see." Mary Virginia looked at her over her bifocals. "You are typically on time and occasionally even come to work early. As long as this doesn't become a habit..."

"Oh, no. I promise you it won't become a habit," Deloris pleaded. "I'll stay fifteen minutes later to cover my time."

This would actually work out best for Deloris anyway, she figured, because she needed to stick around the station until Austin finished his shift so he could take her to target practice.

"I think that is fair," Mary Virginia agreed.

When she finished working her extra time, Deloris went to lunch at Woolworth's Lunch Counter and lingered there until she returned to the station. She had an hour and a half to kill until Austin was off work. She walked into the police department at 3:30 p.m. and found Austin talking with Big Jim. When he saw Deloris, he stood up and walked toward her.

"Hang on a minute. I'll get my hat," Austin stood up, but a leg cramp sat him back down in his chair. "I'll be with you in a minute." He stood up again and rubbed the back of his leg.

"Okay, old man," Deloris kidded. "Are you going to be okay?"

He started walking it off and stopped mid-step to snarl at her. Then he said, "Show some respect to your elders."

They both laughed.

"You've got the gun, right?" Austin asked before walking away.

"Yes, I've got the gun. See." She pulled it out of her purse to show him.

He nodded and then went to the chief's office and told him he wouldn't be back until tomorrow. Chief Douglas barely looked up from his paperwork and gave him a dismissive wave. They left out the back door to get to Austin's car and hopped in before he brought the machine to life with a turn of the key. They drove east for about thirty minutes to a farm near the Missouri River. Austin knew the farmer there, because it was where he and several other police officers went to do target practice and sight their guns. He borrowed three or four bales of hay from the farmer, set them up, and stuck a bullseye on them. He then set up several glass bottles on a fence rail for her to shoot. Austin took the gun from Deloris's hands and started giving her instructions.

"Okay, here is the gun." He pointed at different parts. "This is the hammer, and this is the trigger. The bullet comes out here." Austin grinned as he said this.

"I know that, silly," Deloris scolded. "Remembered my dad was pretty good with a gun. He beat Wyatt Earp with a rifle in two different shooting matches."

"Okay, okay. Hold the gun in your hand and feel its weight. Then hold it with both hands when you plan to shoot it. Aiming the gun is like pointing your trigger finger. Where it points is where the bullet will go. When you shoot, the gun will go up, and that is why you hold it with both hands. The hammer will recoil and could break your thumbs. So don't let your thumbs drift up and get behind the hammer when firing the gun." He took the gun back and showed her, "Hold it this way." He handed the gun back.

"Fire when you are ready," Austin instructed.

Holding it as instructed, Deloris took aim at the hay bales and fired, and the first bullet barely hit the top of the target on the edge as she felt the gun's recoil. She aimed it down a little lower, and this time it hit the bottom of the target. She vowed to hold the nozzle steady to prevent the shots from going too high or too low. The next five shots hit the bullseye. Then Austin set up empty soup and vegetable cans. One, two, three, four, five, six cans fell as the bullets knocked them off their perch. Reloaded, Deloris was ready to go again. Oops, she missed that one. She started again. One, two, three, four pop bottles, an empty mustard jar, and an empty ketchup bottle all bit the dust. Once she became accustomed to the gun's feel and recoil, she was surprisingly accurate in hitting the bullseye and the bottles.

"Hey that's pretty good," Austin commented.

"Of course," Deloris said with a wide grin. "Remember, my father was a sharpshooter."

Why wouldn't she be a deadeye dick, too? Confident in her own abilities, Deloris felt she was ready for whatever fate had in store for her. She and Austin stood talking for a while until the gun cooled off. Once it cooled off, Austin showed her how to clean the gun. He pulled out an oil rag, a small bottle of oil, and a couple of pipe cleaners from a bag he had brought with him. Once the gun was clean, Deloris put it in her purse, and they returned to the city.

As they got into Austin's car, Deloris told him about inheriting David's car and not being able to drive. She watched every move Austin made starting his car and putting it in gear.

"What kind of car is it?" Austin asked as they pulled away from the farm.

"Oh, I don't know. Something Auburn," she replied disinterestedly.

"An Auburn? If it is an Auburn 851 Speedster, that's a nice car. I wouldn't mind driving it." He offered to teach her, but Deloris balked at the offer.

"Look, my brother Clarence tried to teach me years ago. I'm just not mechanically inclined," she admitted.

Austin said, "It's nothing to be afraid of. It's easy; all you need to know is this: you've got your spark control rod, hand throttle lever, choke, carburetor adjusting rod, gasoline shut-off valve, ignition switch, lighting switch, clutch control, brake, and gearshift. There are only three gears — first, second, and third, neutral, and reverse. You must push the clutch in all the way to change gears and let out on the clutch slowly until it engages and you are off. Easy peasy."

At this point, Deloris's eyes were glazing over, and she shook her head. "I can't remember all of that. No, the car will sit until I can sell it."

"You could get someone to drive you around in it. Don't sell it yet," Austin implored.

She agreed, and he dropped her off at Thelma's house.

Chapter Seventeen

David's House

After her shift at the switchboard, Deloris caught a bus and went to 10th and The Paseo—David's house. In all the years she knew David, she never imagined him having a house like this. It looked magnificent. He bought it just six months before, when he thought he was going to marry Lucy and start a family. Wrought-iron fencing topped a stone wall that surrounded the property. Two stone posts were on either side of the gated entrance. Atop the stone posts were round marble finials. A sign to the right of the entrance read, "House beside the road."

"That's interesting," Deloris thought to herself. "I wonder who named it that. It doesn't sound too imaginative." Looking at the yard that inclined down to the fence, she said out loud, "That yard can't be easy to cut."

Looking up at the house from the street level, Deloris saw it was a Second Renaissance Revival style house, a term she remembered from a high school class that covered architectural designs. The house had a tooled, smooth limestone lower level and buff-colored brick on the second level. Two rows of terra-cotta stone divided each level. She backed into the street to get a better view of the top. It had windows wrapping around the top floor, and a simple style modillion cornice with a balustrade above that crowned the very top that could be used as a widow's watch or a widow's walk. She was curious to know if it was, but she didn't have time today to check it out.

The main house was three levels. She walked to the side of the house and looked at the back, where there was a two-level addition. "It was a vastly large house," he thought as she walked back to the front. What in the world did David want with such a big house? "He must have expected to have a large family." She smiled to herself and then felt sad for what might have been. To the right of the front entrance was a Renaissance oriel bay window with one pane on each side and three in the middle. Continuing the Second Renaissance Revival style of the house, the front porch was topped with a wrought-iron cornice, providing a walkout from one room. Behind the house was a detached carriage house that matched the main house's architecture and could just barely be seen above the wall.

Deloris took the house key out of her purse and fit it into the lock on the door that had two long windows on either side. She opened the door and stepped inside. Carefully putting the key in her coat pocket, she then grabbed a pencil and a pad of paper out of her purse before setting her purse just inside the door and closing it. She turned and walked to the house next door and knocked, but no one appeared to be home. She then tried the house on the other side and again found no one home. Walking across the street, she saw a lady outside working in her yard, shoveling the last bits of snow and ice from her sidewalk. She had already spotted Deloris and watched as she approached.

"Hello, my name is Deloris Markham and I am... was," she corrected herself, "a good friend of Dr. David Kerns. I came to check on his house. Well, actually, I inherited the house from Dr. Kerns, so I will be your new neighbor in the future. Do you have a few minutes to talk with me?"

"Sure sweetie. Nice to meet you. My name is Priscilla Hearst."

She said as she stood up and took off her gloves and extended her hand. Seeing Deloris's eyebrows jump, she added, "Yes, my husband, Howard, is a distant cousin to the Hearsts." She smiled and continued, "Welcome to the neighborhood. Come on inside, and we'll have some hot tea. Do you know when you will move in?"

"No. I haven't had time to even think about that. I just learned I inherited the house yesterday," Deloris replied.

Priscilla beckoned Deloris to follow her inside and told her to take a seat in the living room while she got the tea. From her front window, she had an excellent view of David's house.

When Priscilla returned with the tea, Deloris added, "I am also trying to find out when his ex-girlfriend was here and if she took his watch. We can't seem to find it." She was getting pretty good at telling little fibs, and this was just to find out if Lucy had been there.

"Oh, I can tell you plenty," Priscilla said with a wink. "I saw a stocky-looking man come to the house the Wednesday before Dr. Kerns died. I heard him and Dr. Kerns yelling at each other. Later, I saw a woman knock on his door, but he didn't let her in. They talked on the front porch, and then the woman started flailing her arms and yelling at him." She demonstrated how the woman flailed her arms. "I ran to my screened-in front porch where I could hear her say something like, 'You will regret this, and then he slammed the door in her face."

Deloris made a mental note that this neighbor may be a little nosy, but would be an excellent asset to know everything going on in the neighborhood. "Did you hear what they were talking about before she started yelling?"

"No, but I saw the woman at the house again that Friday when Dr. Kerns wasn't home. I later found out he was dead. I happened to be outside covering my yard statuary and bushes before the ice storm."

"Did she stay long the second time?"

"I don't know, but she walked around the house looking in the windows. I couldn't see her when she went around to the back of the house, and I didn't see her leave because my phone rang and I went inside to answer it. One night last week, I also saw a light from a flashlight in the house, but I didn't see anyone go inside. I called the police, but the light was gone by the time they got here."

"Okay, well, you have been very helpful. I'm going to go inside the house now to see if I can find his watch." Deloris put down her teacup. "Thank you very much for your help."

"Anytime, neighbor," she said with a warm smile. "I look forward to seeing you again."

Deloris thanked her again and walked back across the street. She liked Priscilla Hearst and felt that she would be a good person to know if she ever needed help or someone to watch the house.

Deloris unlocked the door again, went inside, and pushed the button to turn on the light in the foyer. The house was so empty, with no life-force. A huge mahogany staircase loomed directly in front of her, and a fireplace with sycamore trim and red brick was on the right. Over it was a wood-trimmed mirror hanging slightly askew. Interesting, she thought. As she looked around, she realized that all the pictures on the wall were askew, and a glance into the living room showed chairs on their sides and various decorative accouterments moved from their dust circles. A porcelain vase lay shattered on the floor. Someone had apparently been inside searching for something, because she could see that things looked like they weren't where they probably should be. Some of it could have been the police looking for evidence, but they wouldn't have broken anything and left it in this state. She walked through the rooms and saw that there was another broken vase and an oriental bowl left on the floor. The sofa had been moved, judging from the imprints in the rug and the pillows on the floor. Chairs weren't up against the table in the dining room, and the drawers to the buffet and china closet were halfway open. The clock that was probably on the fireplace originally was now on the table. Through the doorway from the dining room to the kitchen, she could see that the kitchen cabinet doors had been left open. Maybe whoever was there was the same person who ransacked her bedroom? Or were they looking for David's safe? Hopefully, they didn't find it. The neighbor did say that Lucy was at the house the Friday after he died and that she didn't see her leave. She wondered if Lucy had broken in and was searching for something in the house — maybe she was looking for the engagement ring that was intended to be hers.

Deloris decided she should call Austin and Big Jim and tell them that someone had ransacked David's house. She paused and looked around cautiously to ensure she was alone before going into David's office to call.

"Is Detective Austin Martin there?" Deloris didn't really know the name of the operator who worked the afternoon shift of the switchboard. She only knew the girl who took her place in the afternoons after her morning shift, and her name was Deelia. This wasn't Deelia.

The operator rang down to the front desk and returned to

the conversation with Deloris. "No, I'm sorry he isn't, but his partner, Detective Jim Anderson, is here. Would you like to talk to him?"

She replied, yes, and Big Jim answered the phone.

"Detective Anderson," Big Jim stated.

"This is Deloris."

"Oh, hi Deloris. What can I do for you? Austin isn't here. He is interrogating Lucy, but should be back anytime."

"That's okay. I can tell you. I'm here in Dr. David Kerns's house, and it looks like it has been ransacked. I know your officers were here looking for anything to help with the case, but I don't think they would have left it in this big of a mess. Do you think Lucy could have anything to do with this, too? I mean she could have ransacked his house and my room looking for the ring. A neighbor saw her poking around the house after David died. I think someone should check this out before I go searching around."

"I see. Yes, I can send an officer out to check it. I can't get away just yet. Austin is actually talking with Lucy right now. What's the address, hotshot?"

She gave him the address and said, "Hotshot?"

"Yes, Austin told me you were pretty good with the gun. I knew you would quickly become an expert."

While she was telling him about her shooting experience, Austin got on the phone.

"Well, Austin is on the line now, so I'll ring off," Big Jim said. She could hear him chuckle as he hung up the phone.

"Hey, what's up?" Austin asked enthusiastically.

She filled him in on what she had told Big Jim, and he listened intently. "As I warned you before, you need to be careful. Are you in the house right now?"

"Yes."

"I want you to go to the door and stand by it until I can get there. Okay?"

"Okay, Annie should be here any minute too," she added.

"Good. Tell her the same thing. I'm on my way."

When she rang off from talking with Austin, she stood looking out through the glass side panels that were on either side of the front door. It felt like hours before Austin and a police car pulled up outside. Austin and three officers jogged up to the front door as she opened it for them to enter. Austin told one officer to go around to the back door and check the outside plus the carriage house. He directed another to go upstairs. Then he turned back to Deloris.

"Have you heard anybody inside?" Austin asked breathlessly.

"No, I believe they are long gone," she replied.

"Okay. You stay here and we'll look around to make sure," he said as he pulled his gun from its holster. He instructed the remaining officer to find the stairs to the basement and check it out. He then walked cautiously into the house. He glanced back to discover Deloris was right on his heels, following him so closely he could hear her breathing. "I told you to wait by the door."

"Oh sure. This is my house, remember?" she protested.

With a look of dismay, Austin shook his head. "I don't care. Stay here!" He walked guardedly into the parlor and checked the closet. In the dining room, he opened a door to find nothing but linens on shelves. He walked into the kitchen and turned on the light, then cautiously opened the door wider and peeked inside. He opened the cupboards and the pantry door. When he stepped back from the pantry, he accidentally stepped on Deloris's toe, and she yelped. Startled, he swung around with the gun to come face to face with Deloris.

"I told you to stay at the front door!" he screamed. "I could have shot you!"

"You know I'm not going to do that. I want to see what you find. Besides, I am guarding your back," she grinned.

"All right, but don't follow me so closely. Give me some space," he conceded. He looked in all the big cabinets and doors in the kitchen. Convinced it was empty; he proceeded to the other rooms on the first floor. When he and the other three officers deemed the house secure, Austin turned to Deloris. "Okay, are you going home now?"

"No. I will be looking for a safe now that you are finished. Annie should be here any minute, as I said before, and we are going to search the house again, looking for a safe. Remember?" she said sarcastically.

"Do you have the gun with you? Or do you want me to stay and help you search?" Austin offered.

"The gun is in my purse. Thank you for the offer, but I know you need to get back to the station. Did you finish interrogating Lucy? Don't you need to interrogate her again and Bob Scott as well as Doctors Browne and Johnson?" Deloris asked. "With all of them busy at the station, we shouldn't need to worry about any of them surprising Annie and me here."

"Yes, I need to get back," Austin settled.

"I'll be fine. You can leave," Deloris gestured. "Unless you really want to help us search for the safe."

"Yeah, I really can't," Austin sighed. "I'll leave that up to you and Annie. I'm sure you can find it without me, but be sure to take the gun with you when you are doing your searching, just in case. Okay? We don't know for sure if one of these folks is the guilty party yet," he cautioned. "There still could be someone else we don't know about yet."

"Aye, aye, captain," she replied with a glint in her eye. "Oh, did you guys see this roll-top desk? Did you search it?"

"No, not yet," Austin replied. "It's locked, and we have a locksmith scheduled to open it tomorrow."

Chapter Eighteen
The Search

Once Austin left, she grabbed her purse with the gun and looked around. She needed to get to work to see what she could find, but where should she start? Deloris walked over to the roll-top desk and tried to roll the top up, just to be sure it wasn't stuck, but it wouldn't budge. There were scratches on it as if someone had tried to pry it open, but it was a fortress. She looked under it and tried to slide any pieces of wood to see if they would dislodge the roll-top, but nothing budged. She really needed to find the key. The police didn't find it, so the key must be around somewhere. She made a mental note to keep an eye out for the key while she looked for the safe.

"Where is Annie?" she wondered. "She should have been here by now." Mumbling to herself, Deloris figured Annie was probably delayed because she had asked her to bring the canvas bag she had forgotten and left on the bed. This time, the only thing she had in the bag was her emergency kit, because she didn't want to transport all the jewelry and papers around with her for fear, she'd lose something. Before she could go further, she heard a buzz from the front door. It must be Annie. She rushed to the door, opening it before Annie could buzz again.

"You arrived just in time. I was just searching for a key to the roll-top desk," Deloris said excitedly.

Annie looked around, eyes wide. "Did you make this mess?"

"No, someone was here before me and made this mess," Deloris said sadly.

"Shouldn't we leave and get Austin or Big Jim to do this with us?"

"You just missed Austin and the three officers he had with him. They searched everything pretty thoroughly. Once they gave the all-clear, Austin had to go back to the station to finish interrogating some people. Besides, I have Austin's gun here." She brandished the gun, surprising Annie, who took a step back.

"Don't worry. I won't shoot you," Deloris laughed. "We'll be fine. Let's start in the office and look around the locked roll-top desk. Maybe we'll either find the safe while we look for the key or some instructions of where to find the safe, or really anything that might help us," Deloris instructed as she escorted Annie into the study.

"Okay," Annie said cautiously. Two walls were covered in shelves, and the third had a brown leather sofa against it with two lamps and tables on either side of it. The fourth wall had an enormous picture window that was covered in heavy drapes.

Annie started looking in the sides of the sofa and under the sofa's seat cushions.

"I don't think the safe is under them," Deloris teased.

"Of course," Annie replied, slightly embarrassed. "I was just straightening them, but the key could be hidden there."

"That's true," Deloris agreed.

Annie moved on to the radio/record player and pulled it out, looking behind it, knocking on the wall. She went to the curtains and looked behind them. Nothing.

Deloris sat her purse down on the fireplace mantel and looked behind pictures and mirrors, then examined the fireplace closely. She leaned inside the fireplace to get a better look and felt around. When she stepped out, she had some soot on her face, and Annie started giggling.

"You've got some ..." and she gestured to her face. Deloris wiped her face with the back of her hand, not realizing it had soot on it. The little bit of soot was now smeared larger, and Annie roared with laughter.

"Here, let me help you," Annie gleefully offered. She took out a white handkerchief with blue edging and blue flowers from her sleeve and spat on it. When she walked over to Deloris with hand poised to clean her face, Deloris said, "Never mind. I'll just go into the bathroom and clean my face."

When Deloris returned, she found Annie at the bookcases. They weren't quite full, but still had a large assortment of textbooks, medical books, and journals in one section on two shelves. In another section, a few classical novels were on one shelf. Annie had stopped to read one of the books.

"Annie, we don't have time for you to read that book," Deloris said, laughing. "You can just take it with you and read it at home."

"Oh yes, of course. I was just looking inside it to see if there was a note, the key, or anything written inside, and got sidetracked," she said with a grin. She resumed pulling each book out and knocking on the wall behind them.

They left the study and went into the living room. Deloris saw the fireplace in the foyer and remembered that she hadn't checked that fireplace yet. First, they both pushed on the bricks and felt for any kind of button. Nothing. She climbed into it and shone the flashlight up into the chimney, trying to be careful this time. Nothing. She saw nothing but blackness. Great! Now she was still covered in soot and had nothing to show for it. Climbing out, she grabbed her purse and remembered the gun was still in it from its extra weight. Annie resumed searching the living room sofa and the lamp tables that sat on either side of the sofa. Nothing.

Moving on to the dining room, Deloris and Annie looked under the table and each chair, hoping to find at least a note, the key to the desk, or something, but nothing was there. Annie opened the china closet, and Deloris opened each drawer in the buffet. They rifled through the sparse contents, but there was nothing unusual to be found.

Through the dining room was a large kitchen. It was in the two-story structure that was seamlessly attached to the back of the three-story section of the house. This two-story part of the house was obviously meant for servants because it wasn't as lavish. Deloris and Annie looked in each cabinet and knocked on the back wall under each cabinet. A quick glance at the pantry proved it was fully stocked. "What in the world was David doing with this much food?" Deloris and Annie asked in unison.

A small bathroom, obviously converted from a closet, was off the kitchen in a corner. A quick glance into the bathroom proved fruitless, too. The room behind it was a laundry room with the latest wringer washing machine standing in the middle of the room along with two rinse tubs, an iron and an ironing board. A wood-burning stove with two big kettles provided the heat for the laundry room, as well as hot water for washing and heat for the iron. The room was also equipped with a ceiling fan. Two windows on either side of the back door and two windows on the other outside wall of the room provided ventilation in the summer. Outside the back door was a three-line clothesline. Again, what bachelor needed this luxury? Did he have a maid or someone who took care of his cooking, cleaning, and laundry?

"I wonder if David had a maid, a housekeeper, or even a groundskeeper?" Annie spoke up about what they both were thinking.

"I can ask when I see Mrs. Kerns and search for my headscarf," Deloris offered. She made a mental note to follow up on this.

Deloris and Annie went back into the kitchen. Annie went to the pantry and opened the door. She stood there for a while, just gazing at the shelves of food. Then she removed one can, looked again, and replaced the can on the shelf.

Deloris lifted the latch on the icebox and opened the door. What negligible amount of food in there was spoiled, so she threw it in the trash. The tray in the bottom compartment was full of water from where the block of ice had melted and collected. It was too heavy for her to pull out and empty, so she bailed most of it out into a bucket she found and used it to water some sad-looking plants nearby. This made the heavy tin container more manageable. She picked it up and poured the remaining water into the kitchen sink.

They both stood there blinking at the big gas stove with eight burners and two ovens. The back of the stove rose to a shelf at the top where a teakettle, a grease pot, a pepper grinder, and a salt cellar sat.

"He surely doesn't have anything behind the stove," Deloris said. "But I guess we should still look. Can you help me pull it out?"

"Sure."

They removed the items from the top shelf and two cast iron skillets left on the burners and put them on the kitchen table.

"I wish I had asked Austin or one of the officers with him to stay and help us move this," Deloris grunted as they huffed and puffed until they got the cast-iron stove to move about two inches forward. Peeking behind it brought them no more success than elsewhere.

"We'll leave it here until I can get someone else to help me move it back," Deloris declared. Annie readily agreed.

Satisfied that the kitchen didn't hold any secrets, they found the door to the basement in the kitchen. They headed down the dirty wooden stairs to the basement. Deloris could see footprints in the dirt left by the officer who had checked it out earlier. It was a little creepy with spider webs and, well, spiders in general, dead mice, and who knows what else. She almost lost Annie when a spider went running across the floor for the cover of the shelves under the stairs. Neither of them wanted to spend any more time than was necessary in that space. Only a portion of it had concrete walls with small windows covered in bars on each side of the room. There was a stack of boards that must have been left from when the house was built. Annie hovered around the stairs, ready to run up them if another spider or mouse, or something else came out of hiding. The other part of the basement looked like a dug-out cave with dirt walls and a dirt floor. On one side of the basement, Deloris saw a pile of coal on the ground below a coal chute door. She walked over to it and checked to be certain it was latched and secure. No intruder entered from there. On the other side was a long wine rack with several bottles of wine displayed. Deloris pulled her flashlight out of her bag and looked through the wine bottles and through the racks, but saw nothing. She then looked back into the dark opening of the cave. At the end was a stone wall with a wooden door. There was an open padlock on the door. Deloris started to walk back to the door when she heard a squeal from Annie at the stairs and surmised that she must have seen another spider, mouse, or something else. Deloris quickly opened the door and flashed her light down a long, dark tunnel. She definitely wasn't going inside there to look for a safe, not today anyway. She wanted Austin, or Big Jim, or another officer to go with her if she ventured inside that tunnel. She was happy to leave the space. She returned to the concrete part and found Annie halfway up the stairs. She shrugged her shoulders and shook her head at Annie.

"I saw a mouse," Annie said gingerly.

"I figured you saw something dangerous," Deloris chuckled.

"What did you see back in there?"

"Nothing but bottles of wine, a coal chute with coal piled below it and a door to the entrance of a long tunnel," Deloris answered ruefully.

"Do you think the safe could be down the tunnel?" Annie asked.

"I don't know, but I wasn't going to go down that long, dark tunnel alone today. Besides, I heard you scream, and I needed to come save you," Deloris smiled slyly. "If we don't find the safe somewhere else in the house today, I'll come back with reinforcements and look in the tunnel. Now, where in the world should we search next?" Deloris queried.

Back in the kitchen they found a narrow set of backstairs to the second floor in the house addition. At the top of the stairs, they found three bedrooms, each with a metal bed frame but no mattress. Deloris went into one room, and Annie went into another. Deloris opened the drawer of the small table beside the bed and discovered it was empty. A plain wardrobe stood against the wall with a small mirror on the wall beside it. Deloris opened the wardrobe and then the large drawer at the bottom to find it was barren, too.

"Did you find anything?" Annie asked at the doorway.

"No, did you?"

"Absolutely nothing," Annie responded.

They both went into the third room, which only had a bedframe and a broken toy in the corner. They returned to the primary three-story structure and went into the first-floor master bedroom—David's bedroom. The bed had colors of brown and green, but the covers and sheets were strewn about in a heap on the bed. A chest of drawers sat against one wall, and a gentleman's dresser sat next to it. A large wardrobe sat against another wall. The room had a bay window with a window seat. Annie opened the window seat and dug deep through the blankets, sheets, and pillowcases, but found nothing of interest. Deloris looked under the bed, in the wardrobe, and in the gentleman's dresser. She felt as though she was invading David's privacy and hurriedly looked at the contents. A small drawer below the hat door proved no more fruitful than the other drawers.

"Hey Annie, would you mind helping me pull out this gentleman's dresser and then the chest of drawers? There could be a wall safe behind one of them. I just want to check to be sure."

Annie agreed, and they pulled both out one at a time. "That was certainly easier than the stove," Annie commented. When they moved the gentleman's dresser, nothing appeared to be behind it, but Deloris noticed a piece of paper folded up and stuck in a gap and taped with masking tape behind the mirror. When she took it out, she realized it had something inside it. It must be the key to the roll-top desk!

Annie looked in the trash can and found a crumpled note with the word Arsenic written on it. "Deloris, look at this."

"Interesting? I wondered why he wrote that down," Deloris commented. For now, she put it and the key in her pocket for later. Deloris moved on to the bathroom and looked in the medicine cabinet.

"Did you find anything in there?" Annie asked when Deloris returned.

"Nothing except a bottle of Mercurochrome, a tin of Band-Aids, a bottle of aspirin, Pepto-Bismol, and Carter's Little Liver pills," Deloris groaned. "Don't let me forget I want to take a quick glance in the closet under the stairs, but first, let's go upstairs."

"Okay."

Finished with the first floor, Deloris and Annie climbed the stairs to three bedrooms larger than the servants' bedrooms. In the first bedroom, they found a bed with an iron frame, a mattress, and pillows. It was made up with a cream-colored chenille bedspread and flowery curtains as if waiting for an occupant. Two small tables flanked the bed. A large walnut armoire sat against the wall, with a chest of drawers to match.

Deloris went to the armoire and opened the doors. It was empty. She opened the two small drawers below the doors, and they were empty as well. Annie went to the chest of drawers and found it empty, too. One table had a Bible inside the drawer, but the other table was empty.

Entering the other bedrooms, they found them to be mostly barren. One room had an old dresser in it and a white decorative bedframe yet to be set up with a mattress and box springs leaning up against the wall. The third bedroom looked like a nursery, with a wooden cradle in one corner and a dressing table. There was a small room off of it that was probably used as a small bedroom for a nanny. It was devoid of a bed or furnishings—completely empty. This made checking for a safe very simple in this area. Deloris and Annie knocked on the walls in each room to see if they heard a hollow or distinct sound different from the other walls' solid sound. Nothing.

A large ballroom filled most of the third floor. Deloris always found it interesting that typical antebellum homes had a ballroom on the third floor. There was a room off the ballroom that was more of an attic that held an old trunk, luggage, empty moving boxes, and miscellaneous furnishings like lamps, small tables, and extra chairs. There were also some pictures, portraits—of previous property owners, she assumed—and an unassembled bedframe. Annie searched through these items, while Deloris looked inside the old trunk. She found David's mementos from his childhood and high school years. His high school diploma, basketball shoes, a white letterman's sweater with a big purple J, and various pictures were there, but again, nothing relevant to the case that she could see. Deloris wished David had given her more details of where the safe was located.

Looking up, Deloris saw what appeared to be a hatch in the ceiling to the widow's walk at the top of the house. She didn't have a ladder, nor did she know where David might have had one. She decided that if she didn't find the safe on this trip, she would make a note to bring a ladder with her next time. Although she knew the safe wouldn't be up there since it was outdoors, it would be cool to look at the city from up there though. "I will do that sometime in the future," she thought to herself.

Heading back down to the main floor and the study, Deloris went to the roll-top desk and inserted the key. It turned easily in the slot. She rolled the top back and sat down for a long search through all the papers. Annie pulled up a chair next to her and searched the drawers on one side of the desk, while Deloris went through the papers in the multiple nooks and crannies. In the back, under the nooks and small drawers, Deloris found several receipts for large quantities of Blue Mass and some other receipts for pharmaceutical arsenic with Dr. Jeremiah Browne's name as the recipient. She found some dating back six years.

Pulling at a drawer on the left side, Annie found it was blocked until the top was rolled back. Then it appeared to still be stuck. She tried jerking it open, but it would not open. She got down on her knees and looked under it. She found an envelope taped to the bottom of the drawer. "Eureka!" Annie yelled. "Look at this."

The envelope had several prescriptions written by Dr. Browne for both his father-in-law and his wife, Alice. In the back, under the nooks and small drawers, Deloris found several receipts for large quantities of Blue Mass and some other receipts for pharmaceutical arsenic with Dr. Jeremiah Browne's name as the recipient. She found some dating back six years.

"This proves that Dr. Browne was poisoning his wife and father-in-law and probably David!" Deloris exclaimed excitedly. "Good job finding it."

"Thank you," Annie beamed.

"This mystery just keeps getting deeper and deeper," Deloris quipped to Annie.

She walked out of the study, trying to figure out where a safe could be other than in the tunnel, when she stopped.

"Oh wait! I forgot to look in the little closet under the stairs."

Deloris opened the small door and found a string attached to a lightbulb. Turning on the light, she peeked inside. Apparently, it was David's version of Fibber Magee's closet. She saw everything from a baseball bat and a couple of golf clubs (not in a bag but just propped up against the wall) to paper sacks and various small boxes filled with everything from tools to lightbulbs. While Deloris took everything out of the space and searched it, knocking on the walls as well, Annie disappeared back into the kitchen.

After a few minutes, Annie called to Deloris to come into the kitchen and look at something. Deloris quickly stuffed everything back into the small closet and closed the door. "Look how well-stocked this pantry is for a bachelor's home," she observed.

Entering the pantry where Annie stood, Deloris saw that every shelf in the back was full of canned food.

Then Annie said, "I kept looking at the pantry and then I realized it wasn't as deep as it should have been. There was only one row of canned goods."

Deloris looked outside the back door to confirm that a good

four feet was missing from the depth of the pantry. She and Annie started removing the canned goods and other grocery items from the shelves, stacking them on the kitchen table. When the shelves were clear, they knocked on the back wall. There was the hollow sound they had been looking for in the other rooms. They both pulled on the shelves, but the shelves didn't move. Then Deloris pushed, and a door swung open, revealing a two-feet wide and three feet tall black safe sitting on the floor. It had a combination dial, a keyhole and a handle on the front to open it. Success!

Deloris kneeled down and looked at the dial. Then she remembered, "Darn, I left my canvas bag outside of the little room under the stairs. I need to get it."

Annie offered, "I'll get it for you." Moments later, Annie returned and handed her the bag. She took out her notes with the strange numbers on them. Could this be the combination to the lock L4 56 R3 47 L2 89?

Annie held the flashlight while Deloris tried them. She went to the left four times to the number 56, then to the right three times to 47, back to the left two times to 89. Anxiously, she grabbed the handle and lifted. Nothing. Deloris's and Annie's faces fell. Annie suggested maybe Deloris didn't clear it before turning the dial. She learned that little piece of information from a safecracker when she interviewed him for an article in the paper.

"To clear the dial, you need to turn it in one direction for at least two rotations," Annie instructed.

"Okay," Deloris said, turning the dial to the right three or four times and then trying the combination again. This time, the handle lifted, and the safe opened. "Hooray!" she yelled.

In the safe, they found another letter from David stating that he had uncovered some notes that made him suspect that his business partner, Dr. Browne, had poisoned his father-in-law with an overdose of Blue Mass, causing him to commit suicide. He also may have contributed to his wife's death in the same way, all to collect the insurance and her inheritance.

> *"Hello Deloris, By now, I hope you've found the prescriptions and receipts I gathered where Jeremiah Browne had obtained exorbitant amounts of Blue Mass and arsenic. The Blue Mass was well over the limit usually prescribed, and that is what first caught my eye. Did you see the private investigator's report that Browne had a terrible gambling habit? I included it here as well as an additional life insurance policy that Browne took out on me. I didn't know he did that. We have life insurance policies on each other, as is typical for partners to have, but this one is a second policy for a million dollars. He obviously needed more money to feed his gambling habit."*

She found the letter from the private investigator he had hired to investigate Browne. As David stated, the detective reported Dr. Browne was flat broke from gambling. "And here is the second insurance policy along with the one David had on Dr. Browne," Deloris said. "A million dollars is an unusually large amount of money for an insurance policy; plus, David wasn't aware of its existence. Sounds very suspicious to me," she observed.

In a second letter, David said that his recently developed symptoms made him suspicious that Browne was trying to poison him. He was going to investigate his symptoms further at the library. He stated, "I quit drinking coffee that Browne made for the office. I now make my own and bring my lunch from home unless I go out to lunch with you, Deloris. I have tried to be as careful as possible to prevent Browne from poisoning me, if he is. If something should happen to me, I want you to go to the police with what you find in the roll-top desk and these documents. I also petitioned the coroner's office to exhume both Dr. Joseph Walters III and Alice Browne's bodies, but I haven't heard from them yet."

The letter was dated January 30, 1936, just a couple of weeks before he was murdered. Browne must have gotten wind of this petition and decided to kill David off before he could succeed and tell anyone, Deloris deduced.

On another piece of paper, she saw the words scrawled in big print.

"LEAVE IT ALONE. IT IS NONE OF YOUR BUSINESS."

Then, on other smaller pieces of paper, she read:

"I will get even with you."

On one note and on the other, it read,

"You are a dead man."

None of the notes looked like David's handwriting. Was this Browne's handwriting or was this Johnson's, as Dr. Cramer mentioned? Someone threatened David, and then they killed him? If this was Browne's handwriting, then it could be the final nail in his coffin for a guilty verdict.

Deloris became furious at all of this information that she could hardly calm down, and tears filled her eyes. It was so much information for Deloris to process. When she regained her composure, she wiped the tears from her eyes and turned to Annie with a look of resolve. Annie nodded in agreement. She gathered everything and put it in a small box she found under the stairs. She didn't want to lose them before she could get them to the police. She then put the box into her canvas bag.

Before they left, she and Annie searched for where the person had entered the house. In a small room near the back of the house, they found a window that wasn't quite closed. Annie closed it and turned the lock. "If we had a board, we could block the window from being opened," she observed.

"I saw one in the basement. Do you want me to get it?" Deloris replied with a grin.

"That would be great," Annie said. "You know I am afraid to go down there."

"Okay, I'll go," Deloris said as she left the room.

She opened the door to the basement and slowly descended the stairs. She flashed her flashlight around, looking for any movement. When she retrieved the board, she dashed up the steps, slammed the door, and quickly returned to the room. She didn't like the basement either. Annie propped the board between the top of the window casing and the top of the lower window frame, making sure it was secure so the window could not be raised again. Then, the two young women made sure the house was secure, checking all doors and other windows before leaving to go home.

Deloris looked at her watch and realized she still had time to do one more thing that she wanted to do. As they prepared to leave, she turned to Annie and asked, "Will you take my bag home with you and put it in my room, please?"

"Will do," Annie agreed.

Chapter Nineteen
Dr. Browne

Before she told Austin, or Big Jim, or anyone else what she and Annie had found in the house, Deloris wanted to confront Dr. Browne. She was so angry at what she found at David's house, she could hardly contain her emotions. He hurt David, and she was going to get his reaction to her accusations.

Browne, Kerns and Associate's office was only about four blocks from David's house, so she hoofed it rather than calling a cab or catching a bus. When she arrived, she camped out outside his office door until she saw him leaving for the day. Jumping up when she saw him walking down the corridor, she approached him and accused him of murdering his father-in-law, his wife, and David Kerns. At that moment, Deloris realized she had forgotten and left the gun in the canvas bag that Annie had taken home. However, it may have been fortuitous that she didn't have it; she didn't need to be arrested for shooting and killing him.

"What? What are you talking about? They all died by suicide," Dr. Browne said in an agitated tone.

He continued walking hurriedly away from her until Deloris yelled out after him, "Isn't it suspicious that they all died from suicide? Did you poison your father-in-law until he committed suicide?"

An elderly couple came out of a door in the same hallway and heard what she said. They paused to watch for a minute, then rushed out of the building.

Turning back toward Deloris, Dr. Browne yelled, "You're crazy. Why would I do that?"

Hands on her hips, Deloris told him she had a letter from David saying that he suspected him of causing his wife, Alice, and Dr. Walters' suicides. "Did you? Did you kill your wife, too?"

"You'd better leave," he said as he turned back and quickly walked away again.

Deloris ran after him. "Did you kill David, too?"

He stopped dead in his tracks. "You are crazy! Now LEAVE before I have someone call the cops!" He stepped toward her threateningly.

"Please call the cops," Deloris said with a steely edge to her voice. She watched his face. His jaw tightened as he clenched his teeth and his eyebrows lowered over his steely eyes. She detected that she had finally touched a nerve. He lunged toward her and reached for her neck. "I told you to leave!" He had just closed his hands and started tightening his grip when a man came out of another office and yelled, "Hey!" Browne dropped his hands and fled out of the building. Deloris fell to the floor, gasping for breath.

The man helped Deloris up from the floor and told another onlooker to call the police. When Austin and Big Jim arrived with another officer, they were furious with Deloris for approaching Dr. Browne, especially for doing it by herself.

"What did I tell you about being careful and leave the police work to us?" Austin reprimanded. "Do you have the gun with you?"

"No," she cowered. "I wanted to get his reaction to David's letter," Deloris countered. "I was so angry, I just wanted to confront him."

"There wasn't anything in his letter about Dr. Browne," Big Jim stated. "Furthermore, why aren't you home? It's getting late."

"I just wanted to do this before another minute passed. I haven't had time to tell you two that we found another letter accusing Dr. Browne of poisoning his wife and father-in-law. And there was proof of it," Deloris said proudly.

"What kind of proof and where is it?" Big Jim asked.

"We found several prescriptions for both Dr. Walters and Alice Browne written for Blue Mass that David said was well over the acceptable limit in his letter," Deloris replied.

"Where did you find all of this? We searched his house," Austin asked.

"Did the locksmith get you into the roll-top desk today?" Deloris asked.

"No," Austin replied sheepishly.

"Well, I got in it," Deloris countered triumphantly. "I found the key, and the prescriptions were in there as well as a letter from a private investigator saying that Dr. Browne was broke and had a gambling problem."

But their reaction was not what she was expecting. They were both fuming.

"Why didn't you come tell us instead of confronting Browne?!" Big Jim asked.

"Why didn't you let the police handle it for once?" Austin

shouted. “He could have killed you! Plus, do you have this evidence on you? He could have taken it, and we wouldn’t have anything but your word for it. Oh wait, you’d be dead, and we wouldn’t even have that!” He threw up his hands. Deloris had never seen Austin this mad. “Additionally,” he continued, pointing at her, “I’m kind of angry at David for dragging you into this danger. He knew you would investigate.”

Sheepishly, she looked at them, then lowered her eyes and hung her head. “I know I was foolish to confront Dr. Browne alone, but I didn’t have the evidence with me. I sent it home with Annie. I know I should have told you and given it to you, then waited for you to do something, but I was just so angry with him I wasn’t thinking straight. If you take me home, I’ll give you everything I have.”

“‘Wasn’t thinking’ is right,” Big Jim snapped. Turning to another officer who had just arrived, Big Jim asked him to put an APB out for Dr. Browne.

When Deloris got home, she ran upstairs to her room, where Annie had placed the bag on her bed. She grabbed it and ran back downstairs, where Austin and Big Jim waited.

“Here is everything I found,” she said as she reached in the bag and pulled out the box and handed it to Big Jim.

“I think we should request a special patrol for Thelma’s house until this entire business is resolved. Don’t you?” he asked, turning to Austin.

Austin agreed and added, “Maybe we should request that they tail her too, just to keep her out of trouble.” They both laughed as they walked out the door.

Deloris ran to her room and started getting ready for work at The Ship.

That night, a man came into The Ship selling a miracle cure-all named Devonshire Earth Salts. "It cures pneumonia, cancer, diphtheria, typhoid fever, appendicitis, tapeworms, rheumatism, bronchitis, skin disease, high blood pressure, tumors, and snake bites." He touted his cure-all to the customers.

When Willie the bartender finished pouring a mug of beer for a customer, he walked over to the man and said, "Okay, buddy, I think it is time for you to leave. Our customers are all hale and hearty and don't need your medicine." He took the fellow's arm and pulled him out of the bar. As he did this, all the bar patrons started applauding.

Several of the patrons in the bar that night were in town for the General Motors Exhibit at Municipal Auditorium, which was ending the next day. The radio broadcast that evening reported that over sixty-eight thousand people had attended the eight-day event so far, with another twenty-thousand expected the next day. The Ship profited from its close location near the auditorium, and when The Ship profited, so did Deloris. It was a good night for her. She made a healthy collection of tips, which made her feel better after the day she had.

Chapter Twenty
Esther Hernandez

When Deloris came down for breakfast the next morning, Annie called the house to report the news that Blanche Kerns had been found dead in her bed.

"Oh, no! What's next? Who's next?" Deloris wailed.

"I knew you'd want to know as soon as possible," Annie replied.

"I just saw her. I felt so sorry for her when I saw her on Tuesday, but she didn't look very well. I remember David being concerned about her health as well. I wonder why he didn't encourage her to see another doctor."

"I'll see you when I get home later, and we can talk more if you wish. I just came in this morning to type up a story and heard the news," Annie added. "Oh, one more thing — I did a little investigating and couldn't find that David had a maid."

"He may not have had time to hire one," Deloris said. "He only owned the house for a few months." Then Deloris remembered that she still needed to get her headscarf. Well, she would drop by and give her condolences to Esther and then retrieve it. She caught a bus and headed south toward Mrs. Kerns's house. She rang the doorbell, and after a few minutes, Esther answered the door. She had been crying, obviously. Deloris told her what she had come for, but Esther looked like she should sit down for a minute or two.

Esther started crying and took out a dainty, plain white handkerchief and began dabbing her eyes. "I don't know what I'm going to do now that Mrs. Kerns is gone, too. I've worked for her for ten years. While she could be difficult at times, I still cared about her."

Deloris led her into the parlor and helped her sit down. She tried to console her, as Esther used her handkerchief to cry into and dabbed her eyes again. Deloris sat there with her and just listened.

"When I saw her the other day and at the funeral, she didn't look very well. Had she been sick long?" Deloris asked.

Esther said Mrs. Kerns had been sick off and on for about six months, but recently started getting worse. Then, with David's death, she became so distraught, she started acting a little crazy and getting rashes that made her itch mercilessly.

"So, you found her this morning?" Deloris tried to broach the subject gently.

"Yes," Esther let out a wail. "She was lying there in her bed so peacefully. I didn't know what to do."

"I know," Deloris soothed. "It must have been a great shock."

"Thursday night she was feeling a little better, but with the funeral and everything, I realized I forgot to get her prescription refilled, and we ran out of it Wednesday. So, I called the doctor and asked him to get it refilled. He said that he would come by to see her," Esther related.

"And her doctor was Dr. Browne, correct?"

"Yes. He came by here on Thursday evening and gave her some medicine. He said it was a new medicine on the market and wanted to try it to see if it helped her feel any better, but it didn't help. She became violently ill that night, so I called Dr. Browne again, but I couldn't get hold of him," Esther shook her head. "If only I had kept trying to call him or called an ambulance, but she didn't want me to call one. She said it would cost too much money. You know, she was very frugal. She finally fell asleep, and I figured I would check in on her this morning. I brought her some tea this morning and ..." she sobbed.

"That's okay," Deloris consoled her. "Can I get you some tea or anything?"

"Oh, where are my manners? Do you want something to drink?" Esther offered between sniffles.

"No, thank you. I'm fine. Don't worry about me," Deloris answered. "Please continue."

Esther regained her composure and continued, "I just didn't know what to do, so I called Dr. Browne again, and this time I spoke with him. I told him it looked like Mrs. Kerns had passed away." She started crying again, then after a short time continued, "and he said he would come right over."

"Where is the medicine he prescribed the night before?" Deloris asked.

Esther paused and furrowed her brows, then replied. "I. I don't know. It should be beside her bed."

She went into Mrs. Kerns's bedroom, and Deloris followed her. She opened the bedside table drawer and felt inside. Then she looked on the floor around the table. She got down on her knees and looked under the bed.

"What's the matter, Esther?"

"It should be here, but it isn't."

"And it was on the bedside table when you went into her room to give her the tea?"

"Yes, I remember I had to pick it up off the floor where Mrs. Kerns must have knocked it over, and I put it on the table. That's when I realized she wasn't breathing, and I screamed. Jose heard me scream and came running in from the kitchen. He stayed with me until Dr. Browne arrived and then went back to the kitchen."

"Okay, may I use the phone?" Deloris asked. "We need to call the police."

"We do?"

"Yes!" Deloris answered firmly.

Esther took her to the phone, and she dialed the police station. She wasn't surprised that Austin was there. He and Big Jim put in a lot of hours when they worked a case. She told Austin what Esther had told her.

"I'm on my way," he responded.

Austin arrived with a swarm of officers, and soon the place had people and officers coming in and out of every door. Big Jim arrived a few minutes later.

"Deloris? What are you doing here? Oh, never mind. Why am I not surprised? You seem to pop up everywhere there is foul play. Maybe we should start suspecting you?" Big Jim said with a laugh. Then he turned to the officer standing behind him and instructed him to call the coroner's office.

Deloris sat with Esther on the sofa while Big Jim sat across from them. He looked up from writing something in his notepad and, with pen poised to write more, he said to Esther, "Hello, my name is Detective Jim Anderson. What is your name, please?"

She looked to Deloris, who nodded her head in encouragement and held her hand. Hesitantly, she answered, "My name is Esther Hernandez."

"What is your relationship to the deceased?"

"I am," she paused a moment. "I was Mrs. Kerns's ¿como se dice?" Esther looked at Deloris for help.

Deloris, guessing what she was asking, suggested, "Housemaid?"

"Si, yes. I was Mrs. Kerns's housemaid. Please forgive my English. I have trouble speaking it when I am nervous."

"You're doing fine," Big Jim reassured. "Is it Miss or is it Mrs. Hernandez?"

"Mrs. Hernandez," she replied.

"Are you the one who found the deceased?"

"Si, uh. Yes," Esther answered.

"How long have you worked for the deceased?"

"I work ten years," Esther replied. At that moment, an officer brought her brother, Jose, into the room.

"I found this person hiding in a back room in a closet," the officer said with a firm grip on Jose's arm.

"He is my brother. He works for Mrs. Kerns, too!" Esther jumped up and ran to him, giving him a hug.

"That's okay, officer. He can stay here. I'll talk with him, too," Jim gestured to another chair. "Please have a seat. What is your name?"

Deloris moved to another chair to give Esther and Jose room to sit next to each other. Wide-eyed and a little pale, Jose sat down next to his sister. Esther said something to him, and he replied, "Jose. Jose Gomez."

"Thank you, Mr. Gomez. You aren't in any trouble here. We are just trying to learn the facts of what happened. Were you there when the body was discovered?"

Esther leaned in to whisper something to him, and Big Jim said, "Please, Mrs. Hernandez, we need to hear what your brother has to say in his own words."

"I'm sorry, officer," Esther looked worried.

"Detective," Big Jim corrected with a smile.

"Detective, but my brother's English isn't as good as mine, so I need to tell him what you are asking," Esther explained.

"Oh, okay. Very well then. Please ask him where he was when the body was discovered?"

"He was in the kitchen and heard me scream. He came running into the room," Esther replied.

"His own words, if you please, Mrs. Hernandez," Big Jim reminded her calmly.

"Oh, I am sorry." She turned to Jose and translated. He then said, "I drink coffee back there." He pointed his finger at the back of the house, where the kitchen was. "I hear scream. I run to see."

"Okay. Thank you. Did you get along with your employer?"

Jose looked at Esther, puzzled.

Big Jim reworded the question. "Were you and Mrs. Kerns

friendly?"

"Oh yes. Yes, we were. She give this." He pulled up his sleeve and produced a wristwatch.

"I see. Mrs. Hernandez, can you give me a full accounting of Mrs. Kerns's last twenty-four hours?"

Austin poked his head into the room and motioned for Deloris to join him. As she got closer, he said quietly, "I know you probably found something out, so spill the beans. What do you know?"

They stepped into another room, and Deloris answered, "I know that Dr. Browne was Mrs. Kerns's doctor. I know he was here last night to check on her before giving her a new medicine."

Austin was impressed. "You learned all that this morning?"

"Yes. Annie called me this morning and told me that Mrs. Kerns had died, so I came to see if Esther needed help. She was in a state of shock after finding Mrs. Kerns. Plus, I came to get my headscarf that I left here the other day. I saw how distraught Esther was and started consoling her. Oh, and we can't find the bottle of medicine that he gave her. He was here this morning and probably took it," Deloris smiled grimly.

"I'll get a search warrant and search his office and house for the medicine," Austin stated.

"Dr. Browne probably decided that he needed to step things up and kill Mrs. Kerns after I confronted him yesterday," Deloris's eyes widened with the realization. "I may have been instrumental in his killing her now instead of later." Deloris shuddered and covered her face with her hands.

"That's possible," Austin agreed, patting her shoulder

awkwardly.

Deloris took a deep breath and straightened. "Okay, I should go back in and see if Esther needs any help."

"How are you doing?" she asked Esther when she returned. Big Jim had finished questioning the brother and sister and left the room. Esther and Jose still sat on the sofa, a little stunned obviously, hugging each other. Esther was crying on his shoulder.

When Jose saw Deloris arrive, he stood up and said some things in Spanish, then left. Esther turned to Deloris and said, "They told me I need to gather all of Mrs. Kerns's medicines and write how much she takes and how often. I mean, how much she took." Esther corrected herself. "Then, I need to take the medicine and information to the coroner's office and give them to a Carolyn Bechtel. Then, I need to stop at the police station and tell them anything else I may remember. I am so nervous and scared. I don't know what to do," Esther started crying again, and Deloris put her hand on her shoulder and then gave her a hug.

She calmed Esther down and offered to help her gather Mrs. Kerns's medicines. "Let's go back into Mrs. Kerns's bedroom and gather all the medicine we see. Also, I'll look to see if there is any additional medicine in the medicine cabinet. It wouldn't hurt to take that as well."

They began searching for all the medications. Still, nothing was found of the new medicine, only Mrs. Kerns's previous medicines and empty bottles. Esther picked up Mrs. Kern's hairbrush from her dressing table and began crying again.

"Was Dr. Browne in the room alone with Mrs. Kerns's body this morning?" Deloris asked.

"Only for a moment or two. I ran to get him a glass of water. He said he was very thirsty, but ... why?"

"I was just curious," Deloris replied.

A moment later, Esther froze, then slowly turned to face Deloris, blinking her eyes slowly as a realization settled upon her face.

"What is it, Esther? Did you remember something?" Deloris inquired.

"I just realized something. When I came back into the room, I can't be sure, but I thought I saw Dr. Browne take the medicine he had just given Mrs. Kerns the night before and put it in his black bag. I thought that was a little strange, but figured he might need it for someone else."

Yesterday, Deloris had suspected that Dr. Browne had probably given Mrs. Kerns some medicine laced with poison. She wished she could go back in time and warn Mrs. Kerns and Esther not to take anything from him. "Then Mrs. Kerns would still be alive," she ruminated to herself.

Deloris sighed and continued her search just in case something else appeared. She opened the medicine cabinet and saw nothing unusual, but she glanced down and noticed something sticking out from beneath the clawfoot bathtub, wedged behind the foot. She bent to look closer and realized it was a small vial. She grabbed a washcloth and a toothbrush and dislodged the vial from the corner so that she could pick it up, and wrapped it in the same washcloth. She stuck it in her pocket with plans to give it either to Big Jim or Austin for them to have it tested to see if it contained anything poisonous. But now she had to leave to get ready for work. "I'll come back tomorrow and help you gather the rest of the things and go with you to the police station. Okay?"

"I would like that very much," Esther said with a sigh of relief. "Oh, I go to church tomorrow morning."

"That's okay. I'll come in the afternoon. In the meantime, don't clean anything up except just what you dirtied yourself. Don't touch her bedroom or anywhere else, okay? And tell Jose the same."

"Okay. The officer told me the same thing."

"Good. Oh, one more thing, do you know if David had a maid or housekeeper?" Deloris asked.

"Not really. I went to his home once a week to clean and do his laundry. He was hardly ever home, so there wasn't much to clean, and he ate out a lot with friends or with his mother."

"Oh, yes. Okay, thank you," Deloris gave a weak smile and touched her shoulder. "You take care. Okay? I'll see you tomorrow afternoon." Then she left.

Chapter Twenty-One

Sunday Afternoon

The next morning, Deloris woke up early, curious to know if Austin had gotten a search warrant to search Dr. Browne's house and office. If so, what did they find? Did they arrest him yet? She knew Austin would not be at work today because it was Sunday, so she caught a bus and went to his apartment, where she knocked on his door. After some time, Austin answered. His hair was all rumpled, and he came to the door half dressed - no shirt, and it looked like he had hurriedly put his wrinkled pants on because the belt was dangling unfastened.

Deloris barged in, talking a mile a minute about Mrs. Kerns and Dr. Browne.

"Whoa, hold up a minute. Say that again and slow down," he said groggily, trying to smooth his hair.

Deloris reached into her pocket and pulled out the folded washcloth. "I found this vial at Mrs. Kerns's house yesterday. I put it in the washcloth to preserve any fingerprints."

"I guess we need to be more careful in our searches," he said, frowning.

"You need to have it tested. I couldn't bring it yesterday because I had to go to work."

"Yes, boss," Austin teased.

Deloris stuck her tongue out at Austin, but continued, "Oh,

and Esther remembered she saw Dr. Browne put something in his medical bag yesterday morning." She caught her breath and continued, "You need to arrest Dr. Browne and search his black medical bag."

"Very interesting," he replied, leaning back in his chair. "Sounds like we do need to pull him in to interrogate him and then go ahead and file charges against him. Sounds like we have probable cause."

"Did you find anything when you searched his house and office?" she asked.

"We have to wait until tomorrow to get the search warrant. So, no," he replied.

Satisfied that she had done all she could do, Deloris waited while Austin went into the bathroom to freshen up. Then he took her down to the police station.

She told him she needed to go back to Mrs. Kerns's house to get her headscarf and help Esther look for all of Mrs. Kerns's medicines.

"Didn't you get that yesterday?" he asked.

"No, I forgot in all the hullabaloo."

"Do you want me to go with you?" he asked. "Or drive you there?"

"I don't think you need to. I can catch a bus. Just pull Dr. Browne in for more questioning and let me know, please, what you find when you search his office and house."

From there, she left to meet Esther. Deloris arrived at noon, and Esther had prepared a big meal for several of her family members who were coming to be with her. "She probably feels a little lost right now with Mrs. Kerns gone," Deloris thought. Esther invited her to join them, but she declined, saying as soon as they finished, she would be going to the Indiana Gardens Restaurant where she was working later that afternoon and evening. She asked Esther if she had everything she needed to take to the police station.

"I think so," Esther gathered the medicines she had found.

They left for the police station, and Jose drove them in Mrs. Kerns's car. When Deloris and Esther went to the front desk, Deloris asked for either Jim Anderson or Austin Martin. Big Jim came to the front.

"Esther brought the things you requested. Does she need to take them to Carolyn, or will you give them to her?" Deloris asked.

"I'll see that she gets them," he replied.

"Okay." She turned to Esther and said, "Did you think of anything else to tell Detective Anderson?" Esther shook her head no. "Then we will go back to the house."

After Jose drove Deloris and Esther to Mrs. Kerns's house, he left to pick up the rest of their family. Deloris suddenly remembered that she still needed to find her headscarf and told Esther. Deloris searched around the sofa and found her headscarf tucked into the side of the sofa behind a cushion. Then Esther's brother Jose arrived at the door with several other family members. Deloris was relieved to know that Esther wouldn't be alone that day, so she said goodbye. Esther protested and told her she should stay and eat with them. Several of the women in the group agreed and tried to get Deloris to stay.

"I really need to get to the restaurant," Deloris insisted. "But thank you for the offer."

Jose offered to drive her, but she told him he should be there with his family. He nodded, and Deloris stealthily slipped out the front door behind the crowd.

Chapter Twenty-Two

Compilation

In her bedroom on Monday afternoon, Deloris took her canvas bag from its secret hiding place and emptied it onto her bed. She spread everything out so she could organize everything in her head. On a piece of paper, she wrote a list of the items she found at Mrs. Kerns's house just to make sure they were considered. Now, with Mrs. Kerns gone, there were four murders altogether. She felt it was pretty obvious who had killed Mrs. Kerns.

Deloris made a list of all the suspects and what she knew about them, and their alibis for each murder. She started with David's murder. She wrote the names of the suspects and then thought about what she knew about each one.

Bob Scott:

- Bob's girlfriend Lucy still loved David. Bob was jealous of David.
- Bob threatened David when he found out Lucy tried to talk to him.
- Did he have access to David the night of the murder? Unknown.
- Tough guy, but could he murder someone?
- Would he be cunning and patient enough to use poison? — Maybe, but she doubted it.
- He struck her as more of a shoot-'em-up bang, bang kind of guy.

Lucy McCoy

- Loved David, but cheated on him. If she loved David, why would she kill him?
- What would she gain from his death? — Nothing.
- She had been arrested in the past for stealing. Did David know this?
- Did she break into his house and try to rob him? Yes, probably.
- Did she break into Thelma's house and ransack Deloris's room? Yes, quite possible.
- Did she have access to David on the night of the murder? Yes, she was there at his house and twice at the hotel.

Then, a few spaces down, Deloris wrote the following names and what she knew about them:

Dr. Donald Johnson

- Recently fired from his job at James and James.
- He blamed David Kerns for his firing because David was offered his job before the ink was even dry on Johnson's pink slip.
- He threatened Dr. Cramer.
- He had the knowledge and the motive to kill David, but did he have the access? — Yes, he was at the hotel the same night that David and Dr. Cramer met, and he had an argument with David in the elevator.

Dr. Myron Cramer

•Has a lucrative research project with James and James.
•He was the last person to see David Kerns alive, except for the murderer.
•He was also threatened by Dr. Johnson. No apparent reason to murder David and nothing to gain from his death. — Not a suspect.

In another space, she wrote a list of the murder victims: Dr. David Kerns, Blanche Kerns, Alice Browne, and Dr. Joseph Walters.

Dr. Jeremiah Browne

•David Kerns's business associate had an extra life insurance policy on David.
•Suspected of murdering his father-in law, Dr. Walters.
•Also suspected of murdering his wife, Alice for money.
•Did he have an insurance policy on them too? How much?
•Serious gambling problem.
•Desperate for money to feed that habit.
•He had the knowledge and motive, but was he at the hotel the night David was murdered?

Dr. Browne was still the number one suspect in Deloris's mind. Right now, he was in jail on suspicion of three, possibly four, murders. Dr. Joseph Walters III, Alice Walters Browne, and Blanche Kerns.

Something kept gnawing at Deloris; that something just didn't feel right. Browne planned his murders over long periods of time, and David's was more like a murder of passion. She remembered she had forgotten to follow-up with the maid, Aline, at the Pickwick Hotel. When Deloris went downstairs, she found Leota sitting on the couch reading a romance novel.

"Hey, Leota. Do you know a maid at the Pickwick Hotel named Aline?" It was a long shot, but you never know. Maybe she knew her and where she lived.

Leota brusquely told her, "No! Why would I know anyone at the Pickwick Hotel? I don't work there, remember?"

"I'm sorry," Deloris apologized. "I just thought by chance ..." Before Deloris could finish her sentence, Leota interrupted.

"We don't all belong to one big happy club and know each other; you know. I'm going up to my room to get some peace and quiet."

Having said that, she jumped up and ran up the stairs. She was obviously annoyed because Deloris had interrupted her reading.

"Well, thanks anyway," Deloris said, looking up the stairs as Leota disappeared around the corner.

The phone rang, and Deloris answered it. It was Mark Corbane. He asked if Deloris could come in the evening and help with a special event being held at The Ship. She agreed and left Thelma a note to tell her she would be working tonight. She realized she was a little tired and took a quick nap before going to work. When she awoke and came downstairs, Thelma told her she had fixed supper earlier and left a plate of food for Deloris to eat before she left for The Ship. Thelma went into the living room to sit and relax for a bit and crochet. Deloris found the food on the counter, with some aluminum foil wrapped around it. It wasn't Deloris's favorite meal, liver and onions, but she took a bite before quickly wrapping it back up and throwing it in the trash can outside the back door. She hoped Thelma wouldn't see it there. She didn't want to waste food, but it was cold and tasted bad. Leota was coming into the kitchen when Deloris came in from the backyard.

"Is everything okay?" Leota asked, which was out of character for her.

"Fine," Deloris quickly replied. "Gotta go."

Deloris then grabbed her coat and purse and headed out the door again. It took about fifteen minutes for her to get to The Ship. She donned her server uniform and began tying her apron when she started feeling a little sick. Sitting down, she felt dizzy and started getting sicker. She tried to get to the bathroom, but...

One of the other servers came into the dressing room to see why she hadn't shown up to take her shift and found Deloris passed out on the floor.

When Deloris came to, she was in the hospital. All she could remember about last night was laying on the floor and people scurrying around her. Then everything went black again.

Thelma was sitting beside her bed, and Austin was standing at the foot of the bed. Thelma told her that the doctors said she had ingested some poison, and they had to pump her stomach. Luckily, there wasn't much there.

Austin said, "See, I told you to leave this up to us to investigate, but no, you had to do things your way and see where it got you." He must have waited all night to chew her out. She could see the worry on his and Thelma's faces. She told Austin she was sorry for having worried him. She turned to Thelma and said the same thing.

Austin asked her what she had eaten the day before. Deloris still felt a little woozy, but with Thelma's help, she told him what she had eaten for breakfast that morning. For lunch, she had packed a sandwich herself and ate it after her shift at the switchboard. She only had a glass of water at The Ship but didn't eat her supper.

At that statement, Thelma raised an eyebrow and looked at Deloris with dismay. "The liver and onions?"

"I'm sorry, Thelma, but you know I don't like liver and onions. I didn't want to hurt your feelings, so I pitched it in the trash."

Austin asked Deloris, "And you didn't eat any of it?"

"No, wait, I took a bite, but it was cold and tasted funny, so I threw it away before Thelma came in to see I didn't eat it."

Thelma started to say something, but Austin interrupted, "It tasted funny? Was it bitter?"

"Yes, come to think of it, it did have more of a bitter taste than usual," Deloris realized.

He turned to Thelma and asked, "Was anyone around the house yesterday other than the ones living there that could have poisoned the liver and onions?"

"No one was there. I got up and cooked liver and onions before anyone got home. We all ate them, and we are fine. My liver and onions didn't make her sick," Thelma protested indignantly.

"I'm just trying to get an idea if someone could have poisoned the food. I don't believe there was anything wrong with your cooking, Thelma, but is it possible someone could have tampered with it after you cooked it?" Austin asked.

"No, only me and the girls were home," Thelma insisted.

Deloris corrected her and said that Leota was home too, and Thelma said, "Oh yes. I forgot Leota was there too. She is so quiet, I often forget she is there."

Austin asked Thelma if the trash was still there, and she said that it was. He left the hospital to go to Thelma's house to collect the trash and have it tested. When he got there, Gracie let him in and asked, "How is Deloris doing? I came in late last night and offered to bring Thelma to the hospital." He told her they got Deloris to the hospital in time to pump her stomach, and that she was resting and going to be okay.

A floorboard creaked upstairs, and he heard a door softly close. He asked Gracie where he could find the kitchen trash, and she showed him where it was. When he took the lid off, the can was empty. He asked Gracie if she had emptied it, and she said no, that maybe Leota had emptied it. Then he remembered Deloris said she threw it in the trash outside.

He went outside and hunted around to find where the trash can was that Deloris had thrown the food in. Lying on the ground beside the neighbor's trash can was a dead animal. The lid was on the ground next to the can, and a package partially wrapped in aluminum foil was on the ground next to the animal. Austin turned to Gracie, who had followed him outside. She was staring at the animal.

She murmured, "That's Leota's cat. I heard her calling for

it earlier." Then she started crying. "I don't know why I am crying. I didn't like that cat. It was mean and vindictive. At one time or another, it attacked all of us, even the little girls. One day, I found it in my closet, and it had peed on my shoes."

Austin asked, "Can you get me a paper sack or something to put the package in?"

"Sure."

Gracie ran into the house and returned with a paper sack. Austin took out his plain brown handkerchief and picked up the foil package to put it in the sack.

Then, Austin and Gracie went into the kitchen, and Gracie offered to go get Leota so that Austin could talk with her. Austin walked into the living room. From the top of the stairs, Gracie said, "Leota isn't up here. She must have stepped out when we were in the backyard."

Austin said thanks, grabbed the paper sack, and quickly left the house.

He hopped in his car and took off. About a block down the street, he saw Leota running with her purse and a small bag in her hands. When she saw Austin in the car, she threw her bag down and dashed behind a gigantic tree. He jumped out of the car and ran after her. When he caught up with her, he quickly slapped handcuffs on her.

She started crying and saying, "I didn't do anything. Please let me go."

"Then why did you run?" he asked.

"I was trying to catch a bus. I was going to visit my sister."

"Well, I think I need to take you down to the precinct

and have a little chat first."

As they walked back to his car, he gathered her purse and bag and threw them in the front seat, placing her in the back.

Chapter Twenty-Three

The Solution

When Big Jim and Austin confronted Leota and asked her why she ran, she repeatedly said that she was going to visit her sister. They asked her if she had attempted to poison Deloris? She said no. Then they told her they had found the garbage she tried to get rid of in a neighbor's trash can, and they were going to have it tested.

"If it comes back positive for arsenic, we are booking you for attempted murder," Austin said, clenching his hands into a fist.

She said, "How do you know it was the garbage from our house?"

Austin replied, "We called the neighbor, and they said it wasn't theirs. They never cooked liver and onions, and they didn't know how it wound up in their trash can. Thelma and Deloris both said there was a package of liver and onions wrapped in aluminum foil, and this was liver and onions wrapped in aluminum foil. So, we are confident it is the trash from your house."

"Well, how do you know I put it in their trash can? Anyone else could have done it," she said defiantly.

"At that time, you were the only one home other than Thelma and her daughters," Austin countered.

The detectives watched Leota fidget in her seat for a while. After a long pause, Big Jim got down in Leota's face and just stared at her. Leota hid her face in her hands and cried out, "I didn't do it! Leave me alone!"

He told her they had proof she had administered the poison to Deloris, even though they really hadn't yet. Then he hit her with a bombshell: "By the way, we tracked down Aline, the Pickwick Hotel maid. She told us that a woman fitting your description took coffee to David Kerns's room." Leota froze when she realized the jig was up and lowered her hands.

"Okay, I did it!" she blurted out. "I'm sorry I poisoned Dr. Kerns, but I wish I hadn't killed him. I wish I had succeeded in poisoning Deloris instead. I miss Dr. Kerns." Leota then told them the truth of that February 13th night. "I followed Dr. Kerns to the hotel and watched to see which room he checked into. I planned to profess my love to him. I knew he was leaving for New York in a few days, so I finally built up enough courage to tell him how I felt. It was then or never." She looked at the detectives with pleading eyes. "I loved him. Do you understand?"

"You have a funny way of showing love, Miss Jones. Please tell us more," Big Jim encouraged, glancing at Austin briefly. Austin's eyes were narrowed and his fists were still clenched.

"I hid just around a corner down the hall from his room, and when he left for his meeting with Dr. Cramer, I planned to slip into his room where I could wait and confront him privately. From the hallway, I watched the maid, who was cleaning the empty rooms, until I saw she had finished cleaning Dr. Kerns's room. The maid then opened the door to another room and put the keys back on her cart. When she went into that room, I slipped out of my hiding place and grabbed the ring of keys, unlocked David's door, and replaced the keys on the cart before the maid returned. I entered his room and closed the door softly, so the maid wouldn't hear me. I hadn't thought this part through, so I just looked around the room. Then, I saw his suit hanging in the closet. I took the suit and breathed in the fragrance of Dr. Kerns." She leaned back in the chair, closed her eyes in remembrance, and paused a minute with a smile on her face. People were finally listening to her every word.

Austin brought her out of her trance by prompting, "And what did you do next?"

She opened her eyes and looked around the room. "Oh, well, I saw his briefcase sitting on the bed. I thought I would find his train tickets and take them so he would be delayed in leaving, but I found all kinds of papers and pens instead. Then I saw two letters inside a top pocket. There was one to Deloris that wasn't sealed, so I took it out and read it. It made me so angry." She stopped at the thought. Her posture stiffened in the chair. Her eyes stared straight ahead, and she talked through gritted her teeth. "I wanted to kill her right then and there."

"Yes," Big Jim prodded.

"Well, I would just convince him I would be the better woman for him." Leota tossed her head and smiled resolutely. "I heard a key in the lock, so I quickly replaced the letter and hid in the closet with the door slightly ajar. When he turned around to take the key out of the lock, I slipped out of the closet so he would see me when he turned around. He must have heard me, because he spun around so fast. He looked startled. I guess I scared him. He blurted out, 'How did you get in here? What are you doing here?' I told him I had to see him one more time, and I moved closer to him. When I tried to put my arms around his neck and kiss him, he quickly backed off and turned away. He told me I was his patient, and he couldn't date me even if he wanted to because of our doctor-patient relationship. It would be unethical. I told him I would go to another doctor then." This time Leota's face didn't show any emotion.

"He said I was a sweet person. See, I am a sweet person. Dr. Kerns said so." She hugged herself. Then her voice broke, "He said he didn't love me." Leota started crying.

Big Jim and Austin looked at each other and shrugged. Austin then handed her a handkerchief. She took it and dabbed her eyes and then blew her nose. Then she continued, "I said, 'But you date Deloris Markham all the time, and she is your patient.' He then told me they weren't dating in that sense. It wasn't like that." She folded her arms again and leaned back. "Yeah, I didn't believe him for a minute," she scoffed. "I told him he was a liar and confronted him about the letter to Deloris. He asked me whether I had been snooping through his things. Then he walked to the door and asked me to leave. I tried to talk with him one more time, but he told me in a very gruff voice that I had to leave. I was crestfallen, broken. Can you imagine? He just coolly pointed me out the door and told me I had to leave?" Leota started crying again. "He was mean to me."

"How did that make you feel?" Austin asked the obvious. Then shrugged when Big Jim looked at him with an eyebrow raised.

She regained her composure again but practically screamed, "Well, I was mad! He had never spoken to me so harshly before. I was also embarrassed and heartbroken, of course. How would you feel?" She glared at Austin.

"So, you were angry," Big Jim said. This time it was Austin's turn to look at Big Jim for stating the obvious.

"Yes, I was angry and hurt. It hurt so badly. Do you understand? He was leading me on, only to break my heart." Leota slammed her hand on the table, jangling the handcuffs. "I left, but I vowed to get revenge on him for being mean to me and lying to me. I decided right then and there that if I couldn't have him, then no one else could, especially not Deloris."

"Go on," Austin said.

"Deloris has her pick of beaux. She always had one fellow or another coming to the house to take her on a date, but this one was mine, not hers. By hurting David, I figured I was also hurting Deloris." Leota's smirk displayed how much pleasure she got from hurting Deloris.

"What happened next?" Big Jim encouraged.

"So, after he rebuffed me, I went down to the basement in a fit of rage. I was so angry, I could hardly see. I went to where the hotel staff kept their uniforms and supplies. I found a maid uniform. It barely fit, but I got it on. I planned to steal the maid's keys again, but as luck would have it, I found a set of keys in the apron pocket of the uniform. Can you believe that?"

Austin and Big Jim both shook their heads in disbelief. They were mesmerized by her story. "Do you believe this?" Austin mumbled in a low voice to Big Jim.

Leota relished the attention from these two good-looking men hanging on her every word. "Well, I figured they must have checked out in a hurry. It was lucky for me." She chuckled and continued, "I looked around the room to see what I could use to teach David a lesson. I wanted him to suffer, like I was suffering. No one gets away with being mean to me. No one."

Her face twisted into an evil look.

"Okay," Big Jim answered, slightly taken aback.

"On the shelf next to the window, I found a box of rat poison. Rat poison! It was perfect! With everything coming so easily to me, I took it as a sign that it was meant for me to go forward with my plan. I've seen enough movies to know that I had to make it look like a suicide. I looked around again and found among the supplies the pads of paper and pens that the maids leave in each room for the hotel guests. So, I wrote the suicide note: I can't go on. Goodbye, Dr. Kerns." Then I put it in my pocket.

"And then what did you do?" Austin asked.

"I returned to David's floor and hid in the same spot as before and watched for him to return. While waiting, another woman knocked on his door, and when he opened it, she started pleading with him. He shook his head and closed the door in her face."

Big Jim and Austin looked at each other and said simultaneously, "Lucy."

Leota looked puzzled for a moment and said, "Well, seeing her made me angry at first. How many girlfriends did David have? But I saw him close the door in her face, so he obviously broke this woman's heart, too. I was going to get revenge for both of us." She balled her fists again, pulling against the chain between the handcuffs. "When I saw the maid walking down the hall toward Dr. Kerns's room with a pot of coffee, I waited to see if she would stop at his door. When she did, I quickly approached her and told her she was needed on the first floor. Something about a guest complaining that she hadn't left them any clean towels." She waved a hand as if gesturing the maid away. "Then I offered to deliver the coffee for her. Having collected the pot of coffee and the tray from the maid, I took them around the corner, put the tray on a chair and slipped the poison into the pot. I stirred it with the spoon and then wiped the spoon before putting it back on the tray. Then, I entered Dr. Kerns's room. He sat on the edge of the bed, looking down at the floor. He apologized for not getting up because he was feeling a little peaked. He never even looked up to see it was me. He only pointed to the table where he wanted me to place the tray with the pot of coffee. When I noticed that a little of the poison had spilled on the tray, I quickly wiped it up with my hand before he could see it and put it in the sugar bowl. He took a sip, and I was surprised at how quickly the poison took effect. As he lay there writhing in pain, I placed the note on the table and told him why I did it. He should have loved me, not Deloris," she said, stabbing at her chest with her finger. "When he started convulsing, I slipped out of the room, returned the maid uniform, and went home with none the wiser it was me." She smiled proudly. "No one suspected me, not even nosey Deloris, the super sleuth.

"Well, that certainly is a story, Leota. Is there anything else you want to say?" Austin asked.

She sighed. "I do wish I could undo what I did to Dr. Kerns. He was the best doctor, and I miss him. Dr. Browne isn't good at all. He never listens to me."

"All right, then. We all know there is no going back. What's done is done," Big Jim said as he took Leota's arm and pulled her to a standing position. They took Leota to a jail cell and locked her up.

Both Austin and Big Jim went to the hospital to tell Deloris they had finally captured David's murderer. As Deloris heard the whole drama unfold from her bed, she couldn't stop the tears from falling down her cheeks. She felt both anger and sympathy towards Leota, the poor, misguided, but vengeful soul. She did not know her evil side. In fact, she realized that she really didn't know Leota at all. She never sat down and just visited with her, and that was her fault. Amazed, she said, "This sounds like the plot of a murder mystery book."

Big Jim added, "What a twisted mind she must have. She actually justified murdering David because everything fell into place for her."

"She wishes she could undo poisoning Dr. Kerns but wishes she had succeeded in poisoning you," Austin said, watching Deloris's face.

"Oh my," Deloris was startled at this revelation. "She really wanted to kill me."

"I told her what's done is done," Big Jim said with a shrug.

"That sounds like a line from a movie," Deloris observed.

"Leota said she would have gotten away with it and all would have been swell, but you kept poking your nose in where it didn't belong," Big Jim said as he frowned at Deloris.

"I'm sorry," Deloris said as she shrank into her pillow. "But I inadvertently helped you two solve the case." She managed a weak, encouraging smile.

"Once we got this canary to sing, she just kept singing," Austin quipped. "She was pretty proud that she could confuse all of us and reveled in telling us her story. In fact, she wouldn't shut up."

"Oh, and she confessed to being the one who ransacked

your room," Big Jim added. "She was looking for anything related to Dr. Kerns."

"So, you said that she wiped the poison off with her hand? Apparently, that poison made her sick for the next three days," Deloris realized. "We thought it was the flu." She looked at Thelma when she said this.

"Oh, there is one more thing." Big Jim added. "Leota was pretty angry that, to add insult to her misery, you inherited David's house, his car, and all of his wealth. She cried out, 'How did she get so lucky? That should have been me.' You really are her nemesis, Deloris, and a femme fatale to David."

Austin continued the story, "After Leota's confession, I led her away to the cells. I wanted to lock the door and throw away the key, never to see her evil face again. I decided to leave it up to the courts to decide her fate. It wasn't easy to do, though."

Deloris wondered how she hadn't seen this coming. Why wasn't she able to warn David of the impending danger? She could see that Leota was extremely jealous of their friendship. She should have known that she could become dangerous.

Deloris thanked them for letting her know about Leota. The doctor came in and told her she could be released if she had a ride home. Austin offered to take her and Thelma home, and they left.

Final Chapter

The Recap

Leota was found guilty of first-degree murder and is now serving life in prison. With good behavior, she could get parole after serving twenty-five years.

Lucy went to jail on a charge of breaking and entering David's house.

Dr. Jeremiah Browne was also found guilty of three charges of first-degree murder, with no chance of parole. He was also convicted of the attempted murder of Dr. David Kerns because while there was some Blue Mass found in David's system; it didn't kill him. Eventually, it would have as the dosage increased, but Leota beat Browne in killing David.

There was a mixture of poisons, including mercury, found in Dr. Joseph Walters' body, and an abundance of mercury in Browne's wife, Alice's body. Poor Mrs. Kerns also had an overdose of mercury and an overly large amount of laudanum in her body. All three murders were attributed to Dr. Browne.

The new resident in the medical practice hired by Drs. David Kerns and Jeremiah Browne to cover in Dr. Kerns's absence when he was to go to James and James, is now a full-fledged doctor. He along with another doctor, has his office in the space that was formerly the offices of Browne, Kerns and Associates. Everyone likes both doctors, but Thelma feels like they look like teenagers and are a tad bit young. She just couldn't bring herself to go to them, so she changed doctors to an older man across town.

Dr. Myron Cramer hired a new researcher straight out of college. Dr. Cramer wrote to Deloris to tell her about the new researcher. He told her that extensive research about Blue Mass was continuing in David Kerns's name. The new researcher read David's article on the subject, as well as all of David's files, and picked up where he left off. Dr. Cramer also filed a restraining order against Dr. Johnson, but no one has heard from him since he was interrogated by the police. Someone said that they saw him board a plane headed to California. Good riddance, was the general opinion.

Regarding Deloris and her new found wealth, Thelma and the girls did not move into David's house with Deloris. Thelma said that the house was too highfalutin' for her and she didn't want the girls to get too big for their britches with any ideas of riches living in a mansion. Thelma still lives in her boardinghouse.

Cecilia moved back home to Wyoming to help her mother, who was taken ill. Gracie stayed at Thelma's, saying it was closer to school for her. But Annie moved in with Deloris, as did Evie and Nora Davis. Even though their parents lived next door to Thelma's, they wanted to experience some independence by moving into the big house downtown with Deloris. They liked that it was not too far from home, though.

Thelma rented the three vacant bedrooms to some new boarders, including Austin Martin, who took the room that had belonged to Cecilia at the back of the house. It allowed him to come and go even late at night without waking anyone up. At least he can count on a home-cooked meal there. Thelma bent her rules of females only just for him because she knew she could trust him.

Annie researched the Second Renaissance Revival style house that now belonged to Deloris. She discovered it was originally built and owned by a man named Dr. Generous Henderson, who died in 1924. What would Dr. David Kerns think if he knew that the illustrious Dr. Henderson was known for treating all types of sexually transmitted diseases for patients like Annie Chambers, a notorious madame at a house of ill repute, and her girls? Annie told Deloris about Dr. Henderson, and Deloris said that she doubted it would have fazed David. He was interested in making life safer for all people from all walks of life. Luckily, Deloris didn't have to go into the tunnel to find the safe, but later discovered that it had been used during Prohibition to transport illegal liquor back and forth from the carriage house. Plus, it provided cover for any famous patients of Dr. Henderson to reach his house.

Deloris hired Esther to help her take care of her new house, but Esther still goes over to Mrs. Kerns's house once a week just to clean it and check on it. Jose still tends the yard and flower gardens, plus cleans the snow when needed. It is different now, though; he and Esther get paid promptly by the lawyer's office in charge of Mrs. Kerns's estate, a refreshing change from the haggling they had to do to get their wages from Mrs. Kerns. She left both Esther and Jose a tidy little sum of money. It shocked both of them since Mrs. Kerns was always so stingy before with everything.

Deloris bought Mrs. Kerns's royal blue 1935 Packard Touring Sedan car and hired Jose to drive it for her. That car was more practical for her than the sporty car David had left her. She still didn't know how to drive, and Austin still tried to teach her, but her eyes went crossed at the mention of it.

When Jose was busy, both Annie and Evie knew how to drive, and one of them was usually available to drive Deloris, especially on weekends and evenings.

It turned out that the charity Mrs. Kerns was going to leave her estate to was a scam set up by Dr. Browne and didn't exist. The estate would have defaulted back to her son, but David died before she did. What happens now?

What happens to Mrs. Blanche Kerns's estate and money? All will be revealed in the next book, The Mystery of the Kerns's Estate: A Miss Markham Mystery.

The End

About the Author(s)

Through conversation and stories, two friends who liked old movies, mysteries, and history started talking about writing a book that featured these elements. One friend has two books published about her mother, Doris Markham. Doris, who lived in Kansas City in the 1930s, experienced some stories told in this book. The other friend thought that a detective inspired by Doris Markham would be a great place to begin this writing adventure. As time passed, the friends developed the Miss Markham Mystery Series. The main character, much like her real-life inspiration, is spunky, hardheaded, and fearless. This is the eighth book in the series; more of The Miss Markham Mysteries are in the works. The name Juliet E. Sidonie is a combination of the two authors' grandmother and great-grandmothers' names. Other Miss Markham Mystery books can be found under Deborah Dilks' name.

Updates, additional information, book signings, vendor fairs, and presentations for this book and the other books may also be found on the website:

Missmarkhammysteries.com

Social media pages:

Facebook — Juliet Sidonie and Juliet Sidonie, Writer

Instagram—JulietSidonie

X — @DeDeM68517

Other Miss Markham Mysteries Books by Juliet E. Sidonie

Two cozy mystery books in the Miss Markham Mystery series:

Murder Among Friends

Peculiarities at the Picnic

One short story:

"Mystery of the Missing Heirloom"

Six Spooky Stories:

A Halloween Cozy Collection

Mystery of the Kerns Estate

A MISS MARKHAM MYSTERY

Prologue: The Adventure

In the early morning hours of Wednesday, May 26, 1937, Austin Martin, Kansas City Police Detective and friend of Deloris Markham, drove her and two friends, Annie Bailey and Evie Davis, to Union Station. Originally, Deloris and Annie were going, but Evie begged for a chance to go, and Deloris relented.

Austin is about six feet tall, has blonde hair, blue eyes, and a square jaw. He can hold his own in a wrestling ring or at a fancy dinner party. He and Deloris are childhood friends, and he is more like a brother to her.

Deloris, a self-proclaimed amateur sleuth, has dark brown hair, violet eyes, a knockout figure, and good-looking gams. She is short and feisty, with a love of puzzles, excitement, and has an inquisitive mind.

Evie has light blue-gray eyes, dimples, and long brown hair that she wears in the latest styles or pinned up with a hat cocked to one side.

Annie is a pretty girl with a cute round face, blue eyes, and curly strawberry blonde hair that she wears short in an effort to control it. She has a few freckles sprinkled across her nose. Annie has a quiet demeanor and is often wrangled into escapades with Deloris that she normally wouldn't get involved.

It was one in the morning and the streets of Kansas City, Missouri, were mostly empty except for an occasional drunk, streetwalker, or other people engaged in nefarious activities. The area around the bars, nightclubs, and gambling establishments dotting the Kansas City metropolis assembled all types of human life.

Deloris, Evie, and Annie were heading out on another adventure, but to Monterey, California, this time. They could hardly contain their excitement, especially Evie, about what the next few weeks would bring. This was her first adventure outside of Kansas City, and it was Deloris and Annie's first trip beyond Kansas and Missouri borders.

Austin dropped them off at the front door, and the girls laughed as they jostled their purses, cosmetic cases, and hatboxes. With the help from a Red Cap who met them in front of the station, they loaded their suitcases and hatboxes onto a luggage trolley. They then made it through the double doors. The Red Cap stayed with them to await instructions for the correct train and boarding area to take the cart.

Annie strode to the ticket counter to collect their tickets. She had made the reservations, but Deloris paid for the tickets, splurging for herself, Evie, and Annie to travel to Los Angeles. Los Angeles was not their original destination, but it was a place they wanted to experience after Monterey.

Tonight, well really today, they were going to be among the first passengers to ride the Atchison, Topeka and Santa Fe's newest passenger train—the Super Chief #2/2A. It was the latest, most modern train on the rails, and this was its second week of full operation. It was advertised as the "train of the stars" with all the latest luxuries—even air conditioning. Annie read that Edward G. Robinson, Eleanor Powell, and

Edgar Bergen had been on board the train for its premiere run.

The early morning departure at 02:22 a.m. didn't bother them as much when they considered the possibility of meeting a famous Hollywood movie star on board, or maybe even being discovered for the movies themselves by a producer or director who might be on the train. They had heard of that happening to a few actresses. They could be discovered at dinner or having a drink in the lounge.

After the women collected their tickets, the Red Cap put stickers on their luggage and bounded downstairs with a suitcase under each arm and one in his hands to load them on the baggage cart for the Super Chief. Deloris, Evie, and Annie retrieved their hatboxes and carry-on bags before he left, then walked into Union Station's Grand Hall and took seats on long benches facing each other toward the front of the hall. Evie and Annie sat next to each other, and Deloris sat on the opposite side. Looking around, Deloris saw about a half-dozen groups of passengers waiting for one train or another. She wondered whether any of them would board the Super Chief. Honestly, with the exorbitant price of the tickets and because Annie had so much trouble getting their tickets, she doubted it. It sounded like they were just lucky to get three tickets available from Kansas City, since most travelers started in Chicago.

Deloris noticed a petite; young woman seated across the aisle and a few rows behind them, dressed in black with a widow's black hat and black veil hiding her face. She was sitting by herself, but she continually looked around apprehensively as if she were waiting or watching for someone. Deloris tried not to stare, but her curiosity was piqued. When the young woman saw a man enter the Union Station doors, she jumped up and rushed to the Ladies' room. Once upon a time, Deloris had worn a widow's black hat and veil to hide from the mob. Could this woman be hiding, too? Deloris followed her.

Deloris could hear crying in a bathroom stall. She waited in the outer Ladies' waiting room until the young woman exited.

"Are you okay, honey? I am very sorry for your loss," Deloris said as she washed her hands and grabbed a towel to dry them.

The young woman's hat was in her hands. She set it down on the counter to wash her hands and splash water on her face. She looked up to see Deloris handing her another towel. After drying her face and hands, the young woman attempted to regain her composure. She said hesitantly, "What? Oh, yeah, yes, I'm okay."

Deloris could see her eyes were red and puffy from continuous crying, but there was something else in her eyes—a look of fear.

"Are you sure you're okay? Can I help you with anything?"

"No, no, I'm fine," she answered as she put her hat and veil back on, grabbed her purse, and turned to exit. Then she turned back toward Deloris and said, "Actually, you can help me. Can you look out the door and tell me if a man with a light brown fedora and a darker brown suit is out there?"

"Sure, I can, sweetie. Are you hiding out from him in here?"

The young woman gave a hesitant nod in the affirmative.

Deloris stepped out of the restroom and looked around. Near the ticket booth, she saw a man who fit the description standing and looking around. She went back inside and told the woman where he was. She had an idea: if the woman hugged the wall outside the restroom area and hid behind a nearby column, she could head down the stairs to the loading platform without being noticed. Deloris would walk in front of her until she got to the column and then return to her seat. The young woman agreed and started to leave, but then stopped.

"Oh wait. I left my bag and hatbox at my seat."

Deloris told her not to worry; she would get them and bring them downstairs to her. After leading the woman safely to the stairs, Deloris walked back to the bench, retrieved the items, and headed downstairs. "Oh, great," she muttered to herself, realizing she had forgotten to ask which train the woman was taking and where she was going. She looked around and scanned the row of loading areas but didn't see the woman anywhere. It was nearing the time for her own train to arrive.

Worried, Deloris returned to the Grand Hall and to the seat across from Evie and Annie, where she put the bag and hatbox with her own. How in the world was she going to carry her things and the girl's things too, she thought to herself, but more importantly, how was she going to get the woman her things?

Annie was reading a book and hardly looked up when Deloris sat down. Evie looked up from the magazine she was reading and said, "What's up, Buttercup?" Then she saw the extra hatbox and bag. Raising an eyebrow and cocking her head, she asked, "Where...?"

Deloris cut her off and, anxiously looking over her shoulder, said, "I'll give you the lowdown later."

Alarmed at this response, Evie wondered what Deloris had gotten them into this time. Annie looked up and said, "What's going on?"

Evie pointed at Deloris, then shrugged, and Annie nodded knowingly.

www.ingramcontent.com/pod-product-compliance
Lightning Source LLC
LaVergne TN
LVHW100526110826
845146LV00002B/798

* 9 7 9 8 9 9 4 1 1 2 7 7 9 *